"You don't like me, Tamar. Why?"

"I never said that—"

"Oh, you're attracted to me...physically," Jed continued darkly, "but that's all." If he only knew. Tamar stared at him, her mouth dry. But he mustn't guess, not ever, the way she felt about him.

"What have you heard about me that has filled you with such suspicion?"

Tamar continued to stare at him, her mind racing. "I don't know. You...you've got something of a reputation, I suppose," she managed at last, her voice shaking. She couldn't tell him the truth.

"I can buy that." He nodded soberly, moving closer. "And you aren't prepared to look beyond the reputation, to give me a chance?"

HELEN BROOKS lives in Northamptonshire, England, and is married with three children. As she is a committed Christian, busy housewife and mother, her spare time is at a premium, but her hobbies include reading, swimming, gardening and walking her two energetic, inquisitive and very endearing young dogs. Her long-cherished aspiration to write became a reality when she put pen to paper on reaching the age of forty, and sent the result off to Harlequin Books.

HELEN BROOKS now concentrates on writing for Harlequin Presents®, with highly emotional, poignant yet intense books we know you'll love!

Books by Helen Brooks

HARLEQUIN PRESENTS®
1844—A HEARTLESS MARRIAGE
1914—THE PRICE OF A WIFE
1934—HUSBAND BY CONTRACT (Husbands & Wives #1)
1939—SECOND MARRIAGE (Husbands & Wives #2)
1987—THE MARRIAGE SOLUTION

Don't miss any of our special offers. Write to us at the following address for information on our newest releases.

Harlequin Reader Service
U.S.: 3010 Walden Ave., P.O. Box 1325, Buffalo, NY 14269
Canadian: P.O. Box 609, Fort Erie, Ont. L2A 5X3

HELEN BROOKS

A Very Private Revenge

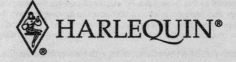

TORONTO • NEW YORK • LONDON
AMSTERDAM • PARIS • SYDNEY • HAMBURG
STOCKHOLM • ATHENS • TOKYO • MILAN • MADRID
PRAGUE • WARSAW • BUDAPEST • AUCKLAND

ISBN 0-373-12021-4

A VERY PRIVATE REVENGE

First North American Publication 1999.

CHAPTER ONE

'OH, YES, Miss McKinley, Mr Cannon is expecting you. If you wouldn't mind taking a seat...?'

Jed Cannon's secretary was *exactly* how Tamar had pictured her from her voice on the telephone, all cool, ice-blonde efficiency and stunning good looks, and as Tamar sank into the proffered chair she felt a nervous bubble of laughter rise in her throat, which she quashed immediately.

None of that, none of that. The little voice in her mind was strong and stern as Tamar watched the other woman glide into the inner sanctum after a reverent knock on Jed Cannon's interconnecting door. You've come this far, you've cornered the wolf in its lair, don't blow it now... But Miss Rice-Brown was so absolutely right for him, she really was, from the top of her ash-blonde bob to the tips of her Italian leather shoes...

'Miss McKinley? Mr Cannon will see you now.'

Tamar didn't have time to reflect further as she rose from the deep-cushioned pale cream chair and waded through the ankle-deep carpeting to the room beyond, passing the other woman in the doorway with a polite nod and smile.

'Miss McKinley?'

The big male figure behind the massive walnut desk was broad-shouldered and dark; that was all Tamar took in initially, along with the fact that the deep, cold, clipped voice was formidable in itself.

'Yes, how do you do, Mr Cannon?' It was the opening she had rehearsed, and it came out like clockwork, respectful but reserved.

And then he stood up, holding out a hand as he said, 'I understand you have some properties you think I might be interested in, Miss McKinley?'—and he came into focus. Oh, boy, did he come into focus...

'I... I...' Don't lose it, Tamar, not now. 'I think there are one or two in particular that would suit your requirements admirably, Mr Cannon,' she said with a coolness she was far from feeling, shaking the big hand for as brief a moment as decorum would allow, and praying her initial hesitation hadn't been picked up by those riveting silver-grey eyes.

She had to keep the businesslike approach sharp and crisp, but she just hadn't expected him to be quite so— her mind balked at the word 'handsome' and substituted 'overpowering'—in real life. His picture had captured none of the latent *power* of the man.

'One or two?' The voice was slightly husky, almost a gravelly texture evident in the slight accent she knew was from his American heritage, and it was very, very sexy, in a magnetic, toe-curling sort of way. It went hand in hand with the six-foot-plus frame, coldly handsome face and piercingly silver eyes. And those same eyes had flickered slightly as they took in her slim red-gold fragility and dark chocolate-brown eyes.

He was attracted to her. She had seen that same look in too many male eyes in the past to doubt its portent. And that was good, that was very, very good—exactly what she had planned when she had dressed with such care that morning. She loathed this man, hated and despised him, but he mustn't know, not yet.

'Yes, we never like to put our clients in a position where they have a choice of one.' What would Jed Cannon say if he knew he was being hunted? Tamar asked herself with a touch of wry cynicism as she smiled coolly into the hard face. Here was a man with the world at his feet, figuratively speaking. A wealthy, powerful millionaire, who wore his women in the same way as he did his designer suits—to complement and enhance his own spectacular image.

He'd already had more women that she had had hot dinners, if only half the stories about him were true, and there was a queue a mile long to be the next female on his arm. Perhaps he expected her to fall in a little heap at his feet? Perhaps they all did? Anyway, she had to be careful. Very, very careful. She had to be different from all the rest.

'Please, do sit down, Miss McKinley. Can I offer you a cup of coffee?' He didn't offer everyone coffee, she knew that, in fact she knew enough about Jed Cannon to fill a book...

'No, thank you.' She kept the smile in place as she took the chair he indicated, knowing that once she lowered her head his eyes would be sweeping all over her hair, her face, her body. 'I have another appointment that is somewhat pressing when I leave here.'

Nice touch, that, Tamar, she told herself as she raised her head with the words and noticed them register in his eyes. He wasn't used to women refusing anything from him.

'I see.' He hadn't liked it, she just *knew* he hadn't liked it, but you would never have known from the smooth, even tone of voice and polite face. Oh, he was good at what he did—you had to give him that. She could see how he'd risen from relative obscurity to where he was now in just ten years. 'Well, I'm interested in what you have to offer, of course'—he sat down opposite her and she noticed how his lean, muscled frame caused the massive executive chair to shrink—'but how did Taylor and Taylor know I was looking for a property in the London area? I wasn't aware you were one of the estate agents my secretary contacted.'

You know darn well we weren't. 'We thought it appropriate to bring the mountain to Mohammed,' she prevaricated quietly, trying a sweeter smile this time. It worked.

'Well, no matter.' He smiled back, and she had to admit the effect was devastating. The harsh, masculine face mellowed, the ice-grey eyes crinkled and the whiteness of his perfect teeth would have done credit to any toothpaste commercial. And it left her cold. She was *determined* it would leave her cold. Her rapid heartbeat, the sudden dryness in her mouth, the rush of blood in her veins—it was all to be expected in the circumstances, and was due purely to the increased adrenalin pumping through her system.

There was a great deal hanging on this meeting, more than Jed Cannon would ever know. She had to get him interested *now*, she might not get another chance, and she had researched her intended quarry very carefully over the last few months.

'I understand it is the property, rather than the specific area, which is of prime importance?' Tamar asked steadily, consulting the fat file on her lap before steeling herself to meet those strangely beautiful eyes again. She had seen people with grey eyes before, but never with the mercurial silver tint this man's had, and his thick black lashes and black eyebrows threw the brilliant gaze into even more prominence, making it quite unnerving.

'Uh-huh.' Again the faintest trace of an American accent was there—due to his living and working in the States for some years after he left university, the dossier in her brain reminded her.

Born and educated in England—only the very best of public schools followed by Oxford, of course, for the great Jed Cannon— of an American mother and English father, he had one sibling—a younger sister—who was now his only close relative, his father having died when Jed was at university, and his mother just two years later. The facts were seared on her brain. He had inherited a considerable fortune at the tender age of twenty-four— the same age she was now—and in the ten years since then had gone on to carve out a name for himself in the world of finance, rising through the ranks of lesser mortals with meteor-like swiftness. Of course his money had talked...

She caught the thought as soon as it formed, a stab of honesty killing it stone-dead. No, that wasn't fair, and she knew it. Fortunes were won and lost all the time in the world in which Jed Cannon lived, and, although his wealth might have given him a safety net in the beginning, it was his own ruthless flair and determination that had made him into a multimillionaire at the age of thirty-four. And if anyone was ruthless, Jed Cannon was...

'And you want absolute privacy, plenty of ground, definitely not a flat or an apartment?' Tamar continued evenly, moving her head just the slightest, so the red-gold mass of curls which just brushed her shoulders in a gleaming cascade of colour would catch the light.

She normally wore her hair pulled back in a severe

knot for work, or in a high but sedate ponytail if she didn't have any clients to see—male interest could be distracting and annoying, or even downright dangerous when she was showing prospective buyers round the more isolated properties—but this wasn't a normal situation. And Jed Cannon definitely wasn't your average bright-eyed and bushy-tailed man either.

'You have been very thorough, Miss McKinley.'

You'll never know. His voice had carried a shadow of wry complacency, and Tamar knew why. He had noticed her movement with the hair, and thought she was out to secure more than just his interest in a property. Which she was. But she knew better than to make it too easy for him.

He only had to reach out his hand and pick up the telephone, and any number of beautiful, willing females would be panting at the leash. But he was going to have to work hard for the pleasure of her company, if he did but know it.

'Thoroughness is our trademark at Taylor and Taylor, and of course the firm is excellent at procuring what the client wants.' It was typical soft soap, but he mustn't even begin to suspect that her research on him resembled a dissertation.

'I'm sure it is.' Again the note of cynicism was there—he knew, and he knew she knew, that her employers were any one of a number of mediocre estate agents dotted about the London area.

'Perhaps you would like to glance at these three properties first?' Tamar asked brightly, passing some papers across the desk and making sure their hands didn't touch in the process.

He had big hands—capable hands—she thought musingly, keeping her gaze trained on the desk and not on his face as he looked at the first of the folders she had handed to him. Fingernails cut short and immaculately clean, no rings, fingers long and surprisingly artistic...

She didn't like where her thoughts were leading, and raised her head abruptly despite her previous decision that he mustn't think she was ogling him. He probably wasn't in the slightest bit artistic, she told herself firmly. In fact she would bet her bottom dollar he wasn't.

His eyelashes were far too generous for a man—she knew girls who would kill for such thick, long lashes—and the chiselled cheekbones and hard, strong mouth formed an interesting contrast... This time she jerked her eyes away to the file on her lap, pretending to sort through the remaining paperwork as she waited for him to finish, and furious with herself when she found that her hands were trembling.

'I actually like all three.' He raised his head and looked straight at her as he spoke.

He was hiding it well, but he was surprised, she thought intuitively—as well he might be. He'd never know what it had cost to get those properties on their books in the last few weeks. For the first time in her life she had employed the sort of strong-arm tactics she despised in others, and she wasn't proud of it. But needs must, and business was business after all. And she had known exactly what to go for—the months of patient research on Jed Cannon had finally paid off, and in a manner she'd never hoped for. Talk about a gift from the gods...

'That's good, Mr Cannon.' She was aware the silver eyes had narrowed at her cool lack of emotion, and allowed the most formal of smiles to brush her lips before she continued, 'Viewing can be arranged at your convenience, of course.'

'It needs to be soon; I'm already seeing a couple of other places this week,' he said immediately, standing as he spoke, and moving round the enormous desk to sit on one corner as he handed her the papers. 'We'll try the top one first. That one has something about it I particularly like.'

'Certainly.' Her voice wasn't as crisp as she would have wished it to be, mainly because of the overall height and breadth of him now he was so close, and the way his pose brought the suit trousers tight over fiercely masculine hips. She didn't like him, she could never be attracted to a loathsome low-life like Jed Cannon, but...he'd got something. Much as she hated to admit it. Call it charisma, male magnetism, sheer old-fashioned pulling power—he had got it.

'Tell me a bit about each property and the present owners— advantages and disadvantages, how soon they can move out, that type of thing,' he said smoothly, watching her as she made some notes in her appointment book. 'Is there anyone who is locked into a chain, for example?'

He made no effort to return to the chair behind the desk after she'd handed the property particulars back to him, holding the papers in one hand as he viewed her from his casual stance, his eyes glittering and metallic in the sunlight streaming in through the big plate-glass window at the side of them.

Don't gabble, don't gabble. Tamar forced herself to speak concisely and clearly as she outlined information about each of the houses he had looked at, but she couldn't do anything about the colour staining her cheeks, much as she would have liked to. Unfortunately the tendency to blush went hand in hand with her red hair, and had been the bane of her life for as long as she could remember. It was useless to tell herself that this intimidating attitude was one he had honed to perfection in the course of his life, that all her data on this man screamed ruthlessness and power obsession, that he was a megalomaniac of the first order.

She knew it all—in her head—but that didn't help much when she was face-to-face with the living reality. Nevertheless, she got through her little discourse without disgracing herself, finishing with, 'But of course there is nothing like viewing the properties themselves. Buying a home is often much more of the heart than the head.'

'You think so?' His mouth twisted, and again the dark aura was so strong she could touch it. 'I disagree—but only for myself, that is. I never let my heart rule my head, Miss McKinley.'

'No?' She knew that only too well, but she kept her voice light when she said, 'You must miss a lot of fun that way, Mr Cannon.'

'Possibly,' he agreed coolly. 'Although that would probably depend on one's definition of the word "fun".'

She couldn't be drawn into anything of this nature— not now, it was too soon—and so Tamar shrugged gracefully, dropping her eyes from his as she closed the file on her lap and murmured demurely, 'You may well be right.'

'As in "the customer is always…"?' he drawled drily.

'What?' She was too taken aback to be polite.

'Forgive me, Miss McKinley, but I feel your response was more of the head than the…heart?'

The pause before the word 'heart' was intentionally

provocative, and Tamar could have kicked herself a moment later when she shot back with, 'You're right, as always, Mr Cannon.'

'Ah…' It was speculative. 'I see my reputation has gone before me.'

'Your reputation?' Her voice was too defensive. She realised just a second too late that he had been speaking generally when she saw the narrowed eyes sharpen, and she said hastily, 'Oh, yes, your reputation… Well, you are quite well known in the City—'

'Too late.' It was very dry. 'I gather whatever you've heard was not complimentary, but I won't embarrass you further by asking for gory details.' His tone stated quite clearly that it was more the fact that he couldn't care less than her tender feelings which had prompted the magnanimity.

'So…' He paused, levering his powerful frame off the desk before offering her his hand to shake. 'You are sure you can fix viewing for this afternoon on that first property?'

'Absolutely,' Tamar said firmly.

'And you will ring me later this morning to confirm?' he continued, as though she hadn't spoken. 'Ask for me personally, okay?'

He was still holding her hand, Tamar realised a little desperately as she looked up—a considerable way up—into the dark, male face.

She was wearing her one and only original designer suit— which had been bought at a fraction of the price second-hand, but still looked like a million dollars—and her hair and make-up was immaculate, so why, *why* was he reducing her to the consistency of a melted jelly? she asked herself helplessly. And why did she feel so *gauche*?

It probably wasn't very clever to snatch her hand away so abruptly. In fact it definitely wasn't, she acknowledged exasperatedly as she watched the cool grey eyes freeze to silver ice, but she knew—as she further compounded the gesture by stepping back a pace and pushing her hair away from her hot cheeks in order to give her hands something to do—that she couldn't have left her fingers enclosed by his warm, male flesh for one more moment.

'I'll...I'll be in touch, Mr Cannon,' she said shakily, after swallowing hard. 'Later this morning, as arranged.' Oh, don't stammer, girl, she told herself disgustedly— this is Jed Cannon for goodness' sake. He isn't worthy to lick your boots, and you owe it to Gaby to carry this off without any hiccups. Jed Cannon was going to regret the day he ever heard the name of Tamar McKinley...

'Fine.'

He was looking at her as though she were slightly mad, Tamar thought with a sudden faint touch of hysteria, and she really couldn't blame him. And she had planned to be so cool, so very contained and in control! Oh, she hoped she hadn't blown it.

It appeared she hadn't.

'What are you doing for lunch?' he asked suddenly, with unnerving directness.

She almost said, Lunch? before she choked back the gormless reply and said instead, her voice as cool as she could make it in the circumstances, 'Oh, I've appointments all day, but no doubt I shall manage a sandwich between engagements.'

'All day?' He frowned, and it was formidable. 'Then

how are you going to set up a visit to Greenacres for this afternoon?'

She had wanted to drop this little nugget into the proceedings over the telephone when she rang him later, but she would have to do it now, Tamar decided quickly.

'I have a number of colleagues who would be only too pleased to show you the property, Mr Cannon,' she said pleasantly. 'Our Mr Richard is a partner in the business, and he can—'

'Your Mr Richard could be the man in the moon,' Jed Cannon bit back tightly, 'but he won't do. I want you to do it.'

'I really can't—'

'I insist on dependability, Miss McKinley—' He stopped abruptly. 'Hell, I can't keep saying that mouthful. You have got another name, I take it?' he asked irritably.

Her stomach was turning over, but she managed to sound both polite and unconcerned as she nodded briskly and said, 'Tamar.'

'Tamar?' His mouth lingered over the name, the deep, husky voice bringing it alive in a way she had never heard before. 'Unusual.'

She smiled, but said nothing. He was going to have to dig for every little bit of information he got from her on a personal level. He was used to women relating their life history at one lift of those sardonic eyebrows, but this was one female who wasn't going to fall at his feet in humble adoration. No way, no how.

'The McKinley is Scottish, I take it?' he asked quietly, when the silence began to stretch.

'My father was Scots, yes.'

Her tone wasn't conducive to further questions, but

she wasn't unduly surprised when he persisted softly, 'And your mother?'

'My mother was French,' she said, a little stiffly now.

'And it would have been your mother who chose the name Tamar,' he said thoughtfully.

'What makes you say that?' He was right, as it happened, but she wasn't going to tell him so.

'The French like beautiful, exotic-sounding names; the Scots are a little more conservative,' he said with sweeping generalisation.

She thought of Gabrielle and Olivia, and couldn't stop herself saying, 'I disagree. My cousins have very lovely names, for example, and both of their parents are Scots.'

'Oh, yes?' His voice was easy, and it was clearly an invitation to elaborate, but she had no intention of doing anything Jed Cannon expected of her.

She willed herself to stand firm, a polite, social smile on her mouth as she faced him, and again the silence stretched and twanged, but this time he made no effort to break it. How long they would have stood there, locked in a strange battle of wills, Tamar didn't know, but she gave a silent sigh of relief when the telephone buzzed after a long thirty seconds or so and defused the almost unbearable tension.

'Yes?' He had snatched up the receiver without taking his eyes off her, his voice curt as he snapped into the phone. After listening in silence for a moment, he said, 'Put the call through in a moment, Teresa. Miss McKinley is just leaving.'

Cue exit.

Tamar nodded briefly, her smile fading, and turned to leave. She had almost reached the door when his voice stopped her as it said coldly, 'You will make the nec-

essary arrangements so that you can accompany me to
Greenacres this afternoon, Tamar, and I would also like
to see the other two properties tomorrow. Any time after...' he flicked over a large diary on his desk and finished '...midday, so please plan your day accordingly.'

It was an order, not a request, and everything in her
rebelled. 'I'm sorry, Mr Cannon, but I really can't—'

'The name is Jed, and, yes, you can,' he said evenly.

She hadn't expected this. Her brain raced, and she
stood still for a second before slowly turning to face him.
This was not how it should have happened. He was supposed to have had his appetite whetted by her apparent
uninterest—the proverbial sprat to catch a mackerel—
and then he would do all the running while she gra-
ciously made the odd concession now and again. He
wasn't supposed to meet her head-on like a ten-ton truck.
But he had. And, thinking about it, she couldn't afford
to take any risks at this early stage of the game. The
prey was still a long, long way off from the snare.

'Of course, if you insist...' Her smile had all the
warmth of an arctic winter, and she didn't have to act
at all.

'I do.' It was uncompromising.

'Then I'll see you later this afternoon.' He was pure,
undiluted arrogance, she told herself testily as she nodded politely and left the room. A man who was used to
clicking his fingers and seeing the rest of the world
jump—through hoops, if necessary. But—and here her
heart stopped, before galloping on furiously—she had
put out the bait and he had taken it hook, line and sinker.
She was in his life—only just—but in nevertheless.
Battle could commence.

She shut the door behind her very quietly, and then

stood for a few seconds willing her racing heartbeat to calm down. Control, control—it was all about control. As long as she remembered that, she would do just fine.

She pretended to check through the papers in the file as she remained standing in Jed Cannon's secretary's plush office; standing was all she could manage just at that moment. Reaction had set in, walking was quite beyond her, and the thought of falling in a heap just outside his quarters did not appeal.

'Is everything all right? You haven't left anything...?' The beautiful Miss Rice-Brown looked up from her word processor after a time, and the gracious expression on the lovely face was just the spur Tamar needed to get moving again.

'No, I'm just making sure,' Tamar said evenly. 'There's nothing worse than getting back to the office and finding something has been mislaid, but everything seems to be here. Mr Cannon has asked me to phone later with details about a viewing I'm setting up for this afternoon.'

'Right.' The secretary clearly wasn't overly interested, inclining her head absently before her glance returned to the screen. 'No problem.'

Not for you, maybe, Tamar thought with a touch of wry self-mockery as she waded through the carpet again to the outer door, stepping into the silent corridor outside and walking over to the lift with a dignity she was far from feeling.

Had she bitten off more than she could chew, here? she asked herself nervously, the lift whisking her down to the ground floor of the Cannon Express building before she could blink. Very probably, but then, nothing ventured—nothing gained...

The warm, sluggish air was portentous of another baking hot August day, but as Tamar stepped from the cool air-conditioned building into what resembled an oven her mind was not on the weather.

She had vowed, all those months ago now, that one day she would have her day with Jed Cannon and confront him with the near-fatal results of his ruthlessness, and if nothing else she was a woman of her word. But she had realised very early on that she needed to do more than *tell* him. That would have been water off a duck's back as far as this man was concerned, and it was doubtful if he would have given her a moment's thought afterwards.

No, she needed to get into Jed Cannon's head, establish herself as a person in her own right before she let rip, and if she could make him fall for her, however carnal such an attraction would be with a man like him, it was all to the good. She would rather die than let him touch her, but he didn't know that.

She decided she was still feeling a mite too fragile after the encounter she had psyched herself up for for days to contemplate the push and shove of the tube, so opted for the luxury of a taxi back to the office, settling in the cavernous depths and giving the driver the address of Taylor and Taylor before she allowed her mind to transport her back to that morning in February, six months ago.

The phone call had come when she was in the shower, and she had padded into the small sitting room of her one-bedroomed flat in Chelsea, expecting Richard or Fiona's voice to be on the other end of the line. But it hadn't proved to be one of the young, dynamic and recently married Taylors who had spoken.

'Tamar? Oh, Tamar, thank goodness. I thought you might have already left for the office. I... Oh, Tamar...'

'Aunt Prudence?' Tamar had never heard her normally vivacious and bubbly aunt so upset, and it frightened her. 'What is it? What's wrong?' she asked anxiously.

There was silence for a moment, followed by the sound of sniffling and snuffling, and then her aunt said, her whisper thick with tears, 'It's Gabrielle. She...she's in hospital.'

'Gaby's in hospital?' Tamar had hardly been able to believe it. She had only spoken to her cousin—who was more like a sister than anything else, the two girls having been brought up together from the age of five, when Tamar's own parents had been killed in a train accident in her mother's native France—the night before, and Gabrielle had been fine then. In fact, she'd been on top of the world—wildly, ecstatically happy... 'What's happened, Aunt Prudence? Has there been an accident?' Tamar prompted urgently, her voice shaking.

'Not exactly.' And then her aunt totally amazed and bewildered her when she wailed at the top of her voice, 'Oh, Tamar, I wish she *had* had an accident; I could cope with that. But this! This is awful.'

'What's awful?' Tamar was trying—very hard—to keep her patience. Her aunt had never been a person who could cope with any sort of pressure, all the family knew that, and made allowances, but when the only sound from the other end of the phone was loud sobs that went on and on, Tamar said at last, her voice sharp, 'Aunt Prudence, answer me. What's so awful?' and then, when no answer was immediately forthcoming, 'Where's Uncle Jack? *Aunt Prudence, where is Uncle Jack?*'

'He's…he's at the hospital with…with Gabrielle. They said…the doctor said I was upsetting her and it would be better if I came home and got…got some rest.'

Even in her aunt's obvious distress a note of affronted pride was detectable, and Tamar could imagine how the doctor's suggestion had gone down with her aunt.

'She…Gabrielle took some sleeping tablets,' her aunt sobbed. 'A whole bottle full that I had in the cupboard from when your uncle Jack had shingles and couldn't sleep.'

'*Gaby?*' Tamar exclaimed shrilly, her brain refusing to accept what her ears were hearing. 'Aunt Prudence, you're saying Gaby tried to commit suicide?'

'Yes, she did—she did. She said so herself after they had pumped her stomach out.'

'But why? Why on earth would she do something like that?' Tamar asked shakily. 'I only spoke to her yesterday, and she was over the moon about Ronald and making plans…' She caught herself abruptly. This wouldn't help her aunt. She had to find out the facts as quickly as she could, and, Prudence being Prudence, that would be difficult enough. She loved her aunt dearly, but she had to be one of the giddiest people on the face of the earth.

'Aunt Prudence, is Gaby all right? Physically, I mean?' she asked quietly, willing herself to sound calm despite the turmoil within.

'I think so, but she wouldn't talk to us,' her aunt wailed plaintively. 'She said…she said she just wanted to be alone.' The sobs that were interrupting her aunt's words were of a pitch to make Tamar's ears ring, and it was at that point Tamar told her aunt she would be coming up to Scotland on the next train, and that she would speak further with her then.

Later that evening she had learnt the full facts from Gabrielle herself. Her cousin, her sweet, gentle and hopelessly naive cousin, was pregnant, and the man in question was Jed Cannon's brother-in-law. Not that Gabrielle had known her beau was married until the evening before, when Jed Cannon himself strode into the hotel restaurant where they were having dinner, and verbally ripped Gabrielle apart in front of a crowd of interested and goggle-eyed spectators, before leaving again with a crestfallen Ronald in tow.

And then, later that night, with Tamar holding her cousin's hand, Gabrielle had lost her baby.

ing up to Scotland on the next train, and that she would
speak further with her then.

Later that evening she had learnt the full facts from
Craillot, briefly. Her cousin, her sweet, gentle and
hopelessly naïve sister, had been married, and the cash in
question was Jed Cannon's brother-in-law. Not that

CHAPTER TWO

THE house Jed Cannon had opted to view first was a
beauty. Eight bedrooms, six bathrooms, three reception
rooms, huge study, enormous sun lounge overlooking
the covered swimming pool—the list of attributes was
endless. The price took a while to say too, with all the
noughts it necessitated...

Tamar met him outside the towering nine-foot wall
surrounding the property on the outskirts of Windsor,
making sure she was there and waiting in plenty of time.
He had offered her a lift when she had phoned earlier
with details of the meeting, but she had refused, insisting
she would make her own way, due to a previous appointment meaning she would be in the area. It was a
lie, and the exorbitant taxi fare was just punishment.

She saw the Mercedes the second it rounded the corner in the far distance, the shimmering heat turning the
magnificent car to fluid bronze, but waited until it was
almost level with her before she spoke into the little box
on the gate, stating their names and the reason for their
visit to Greenacres. The gates opened immediately.

'Hop in.'

Jed Cannon was in the back of the vehicle, a host of
papers scattered around him as he worked away on a
small computer, and he leant across to open the far door
for her, the chauffeur sitting impassively in his glass-
partitioned isolation.

'Thank you.' It was a little breathless, but the overall

authority of him was magnified rather than lessened by the sight of him working, shirtsleeves rolled up and his tie loose round his collar, in the confined space.

'Where's your car?' he asked abruptly as she closed her door and settled down in the luxurious depths.

Her little old banger had failed its MOT the week before, and at present was in a car hospital having major surgery— something she could ill afford—but she wasn't going to tell him all that. 'Flat tyre,' she replied economically. It was true, in a way, but there were about a hundred and one other defects that were being attended to at the same time.

'And you haven't got a back-up?'

No, and she didn't have a Mercedes, a vintage Rolls, and a snazzy little Ferrari either. Unlike him. Perhaps three cars per multimillionaire wasn't too excessive, but it had still grated when she'd first discovered it, and it rankled even more right now.

'No, I haven't,' she replied shortly, her chin rising a notch. 'Few working girls have, I should imagine.'

There was silence for a moment and then, 'I'm sorry, Tamar, I put that incredibly badly.'

His voice was soft and genuine, and as she glanced at him she saw he was truly embarrassed.

'What I meant was, I would have thought the firm you work for would have provided a vehicle for just such an emergency,' he said quietly. 'A car must be pretty essential for your day to day business?'

'It helps.' She was flustered, and hot and sticky—she had been waiting fifteen minutes for his car to arrive, so nervous had she been of being late, and there had been no shade from the fierce afternoon sun—but it was the look on his face and the softness of his voice rather than the heat which was making her uncomfortable.

She inclined her head slightly now, her voice mellowing as she said, 'It just happened that everyone needed their own car today, and there isn't a pool vehicle—not yet at any rate,' she added hastily. The last thing she wanted to do was give Jed Cannon the impression that Taylor and Taylor was just a little tinpot kind of business. 'But Richard and Fiona are working on it,' she said positively.

'And they are?' he asked expressionlessly.

'Taylor and Taylor.'

'Right.'

Oh, damn, what was he thinking now? She risked a sidelong glance from under her eyelashes as the beautiful car nosed its way along the winding tree-lined drive towards the palatial house some hundred yards away. Did he think Taylor and Taylor weren't big enough to handle this kind of property, that they were cowboys, or—?

'So, most of the ground is at the front of the house, with just the swimming pool and tennis court at the back?' Jed asked quietly, raising his head from his work and leaning back in the seat as he spoke.

'Yes.' Oh, she should have been giving him the sales pitch rather than daydreaming, Tamar cautioned herself irritably, and she went on to list the rare trees and flowers the garden boasted.

She continued to point out each advantageous feature of the property—the genuine solid oak beams in the reception rooms, the wonderful stained glass windows in the entrance hall and on the first and second floor landings, and so on—and by the time they had finished the inspection she had spoken herself almost hoarse.

It hadn't helped that the owner—an aristocratic and hopelessly dotty old colonel-type, who had more money than sense—had completed the tour with them, helpfully pointing out the rising damp in the study, the crumbling brickwork in the west wing, and the failing filtering system in the pool.

She had sensed more than once that Jed Cannon was being vastly entertained. There was something about the studiously straight face and faintly strangled note to his voice that suggested smothered amusement—especially when she found herself arguing with the owner on the merits of a south-facing garden— and when they stepped out of the front door again, after the requisite sherry and dry biscuits, Tamar really didn't know whether she wanted to laugh or cry.

She did neither, inclining her head towards Jed as they walked across the scrunchy drive towards the Mercedes and saying, without any preamble, 'Well, did you like it?' her voice flat.

'Very much.' The silver eyes were positively wicked as he added, 'And Gerald Biggsley-Brown proved to be a very honest and upright individual, don't you think?'

She glanced at him sharply, but the handsome face was bland and innocent—too bland and too innocent.

'Yes, he's very nice,' Tamar said primly. Why, oh, why, had she started this? She was way out of her league here. How on earth could she ever get a man like Jed Cannon to fancy her anyway? She must have been mad. But she *would* tell him what she thought of him; she could still do that at least.

'Okay, set the ball rolling,' Jed said easily.

'*What?*'

Tamar stopped stock-still in the middle of the horseshoe forecourt, so that Jed had actually walked on a few paces before he realised she wasn't with him. He turned to face her, taking in the wide dark eyes and partly open mouth with more secret amusement.

'What did you say?' she asked again.

'I said, set the ball rolling—start the negotiations,' he replied patiently. 'However you want to describe it.'

'But…but what about the damp, and the brickwork and…everything?' she stuttered disbelievingly.

'Tamar, are you trying to sell me this house or do a hatchet job?' Jed drawled drily. 'If you insist, I'll sacrifice some more of my valuable time to traipse around a few properties, but the end result would be the same. I like this house. I want it—at the right price of course— and I shan't change my mind about that. I've always prided myself on being a man who knows what he wants when he sees it, and then acquiring it. I've seen it.'

'You have?' She suddenly realised how hopelessly unprofessional she must sound, and forced a bright, positive note into her voice as she added, 'Of course you have. This is a wonderful house. The oak beams—'

'Were pointed out masterfully, along with the stained glass windows, the new fitted kitchen, and, of course, the south-facing garden.'

He was laughing at her, she knew it, but she was too surprised at the easy sale—and what a sale—to be angry. The commission she would make on this one deal was more than she normally earned in months.

'Now, shall we sit in the comfort of the car while we discuss a few terms and conditions? It must be all of eighty in the shade out here,' he pointed out matter-of-factly.

'Oh, yes, of course.' She found herself almost gam-

bolling along at his side before she checked herself
sharply. This was Jed Cannon. *Jed Cannon.* The sale
was great, of course it was—'tasty' wasn't the word—
but there was more at stake here than filthy lucre. And
in one way this had all been too easy. There would be
no reason, once the sale was going through, for her ever
to darken Jed Cannon's door again, and that wasn't at
all what she had planned.

Once in the car, he turned to her, after tapping the
glass for the chauffeur to drive off, and smiled. She
wished he hadn't. It had been bad enough earlier in the
office, but here, in this confined space, with the faint
smell of expensive aftershave teasing her nostrils and the
dark, latent power of the man seeming to strain against
a precarious leash, it was positively devastating.

'Now...' He leant back casually in the seat, one arm
stretched along the back of the leather upholstery and
the silver eyes narrowed against the white sunlight. 'That
brickwork...'

He detailed several matters needing expert attention—
most of which had been pointed out by the good Gerald
Biggsley-Brown, bless him, Tamar thought balefully—
before finishing with, 'They can either be rectified by
the present owner before I take possession, or by me,
with estimates reducing the asking price by an agreed
amount. I'm not fussy. And of course all this is subject
to survey and the normal formalities,' he said crisply.

'Of course,' Tamar agreed carefully.

'And I want this completed fast—no hiccups, no de-
lays. If Gerald can't get the work done in the next two
weeks, I can.'

She didn't doubt that Jed Cannon could do anything
he set his mind to, but *two weeks*? 'But the survey and

everything?' Tamar stared at him in disbelief. 'These
things take time, Mr Cannon. Once you've reached an
agreement with the owner—'

He interrupted her faintly dazed voice coolly. 'The
guy already has the little seaside place he's moving to—'
Tamar wouldn't have described Mr Biggsley-Brown's
seven hundred thousand pounds' worth of beautiful holiday home in that way, but no matter '—so he could
move out tomorrow if he wants. He said so. There are
no mortgage complications on his side or mine, and I
can get my people in to do the survey tomorrow morning
if necessary.'

How the other half live. How the other half *live*,
Tamar thought bemusedly.

'I want to get a place near London quickly—there
are…family complications that make it important—
okay? So, let's all pull our fingers out and get cracking.'

'Yes, right.' She was still shell-shocked—that was the
only excuse she could think of afterwards for her next
words, which were a big, *big* gaffe. 'But I thought you
had an apartment in Kensington anyway?' she said do-
pily.

'Did you…?'

The metallic gaze had turned to bright steel and was
at variance with the almost lazy tone of voice, but Tamar
was looking straight into his eyes, and they woke her up
like nothing else could have done.

'Have you been doing some homework on me, Miss
Tamar McKinley?' he asked thoughtfully.

'No, no, not really.' She had always been hopeless at
lying, her tendency to metamorphose into a beetroot was
a dead give-away, and now, as she felt herself burn with
colour, she knew she had to retrieve the situation fast.

'Well…' She allowed the merest embarrassed pause before she lowered her eyes and said hesitantly, 'The sort
of property you're interested in *does* cost a great deal of
money, Mr Cannon. The firm prefers a lit-
tle…investigation in those circumstances, to make sure
the client is not disappointed at the last moment by a
buyer who simply can't meet the required asking price.'

'How thorough.' It was cool and even, and as Tamar
raised her eyes she couldn't gauge a thing from the expressionless face in front of her. 'And this is normal
practice?' he asked softly.

'In deals of this calibre, yes,' she said quietly. 'We
like to feel that if at any time in the future you decided
to move again, the sort of service we provide would
prompt you to contact us before any other firm.'

'And what else is included in the…service you provide?'

It could have meant exactly what it said at face value,
but there was the merest inflexion in the tone that told
Tamar he was flirting with her. Carefully, obliquely,
even, but there was something there, and she had to be
very very circumspect now. She couldn't afford to make
another mistake like the one she had just made.

She smiled gently, listing all the pros of dealing with
Taylor and Taylor one by one, at the same time allowing
her eyes to give him just the faintest of come-ons.

The Mercedes pulled up outside Taylor and Taylor—
where Jed had offered to take her—at just gone four,
and she prayed he wouldn't suggest coming in and meeting Richard and Fiona. The shop premises didn't look
too bad on the outside, but if he came in and saw just
how small the set-up was, he might suspect they didn't
normally deal in seven-figure negotiations. But he didn't.

Why would he? she asked herself once she was out of the car and raising her hand to him as the dark gold Mercedes glided away into mainstream traffic. Men of his wealth and importance weren't exactly desperate to meet the minions below them.

'Oh, *wow*!' Fiona met her at the door and it was obvious she had been watching out of the window. 'That was him, I take it? Jed Cannon? And look at that car! I bet you didn't even know you were on the road.'

'It's a bit different to my little jalopy,' Tamar agreed, with a rueful grin at Fiona's avaricious face. She loved Fiona and Richard—she had been at university with them both, and they had helped her through a rough patch in her life then and continued to be steadfast friends—but sometimes the fierce ambition and ruthless intent to succeed that the couple shared left her cold.

They would make a name for themselves in the field they had chosen; she didn't doubt that for a minute, in spite of estate agents being ten a penny in the London area. And that was good, just fine, Tamar told herself as she entered the office and turned to answer the hundred and one questions Fiona was throwing at her. But there was more to life than work. Richard and Fiona genuinely enjoyed working from dawn to dusk, six, sometimes seven days a week, and, as neither of them wanted children, they had decided to sink all their time and money, along with their hearts and souls, into their joint career.

But she wasn't like that. She wanted a home of her own one day when the time was right, with a partner who loved her, and a family, dogs, cats...maybe a chicken or two pecking in the backyard and a pony in a field close by for the kids to ride on? It was a pipe dream, or most of it was, at any rate, but if you didn't dream, what was there? Of course, to form a relationship with a man you had to be prepared to date now and again, and she wasn't there yet, but she was getting better...

'*Well?*' She came back to the real world to see Fiona positively hopping with eager impatience. 'How did it go? Did he display any interest? *Talk* to me, Tamar.'

'He wants it,' Tamar said off-handedly, enjoying the moment.

'He...? He doesn't! He doesn't, does he? Really? For definite?' Fiona gabbled enthusiastically, for once not at all like her normal cool, sophisticated self.

'Absolutely.' Tamar nodded, before laughing out loud. 'And I'm looking forward to a nice long holiday somewhere hot with all that commission.'

'Oh, you've earnt it—you've definitely earnt it,' Fiona agreed happily. 'If we can get a few more clients like him, we're laughing. And to think all this came about because you had lunch with Carol at Webster and Hartman! That'll teach her to boast about how well their firm are doing compared to ours.'

'I feel a bit mean about that actually—'

'Nonsense.' Fiona interrupted Tamar's subdued voice in her normal forceful manner. 'All's fair in love and war, girl, and don't you forget it. You went out and got those three properties you showed him on our books, didn't you? It was your enterprise and push that did that. You deserve to make a killing. It's the first time I've seen you so determined about anything for ages.'

'Ages' translated into five years, Tamar thought wryly, as she gazed at this bright, attractive friend of hers, who was known for her plain speaking.

'And anyway, Carol shouldn't have mentioned Jed Cannon if she didn't expect us to go for a bite of the same cherry,' Fiona finished with a decisive nod of her head. 'I wouldn't expect you or Tim—' Tim being the other employee of the firm '—to sound off about who we've got on our books and who we haven't. And you told Carol you were going to try for Jed Cannon. That's more than she would have done if the position had been reversed. No, you did very well. You've obviously got the right touch with millionaires.'

'Obviously.' But he hadn't asked for her telephone number, or suggested a date, and she had so wanted to get under his skin a bit before she told him exactly what she thought of him. He had treated Gaby like dirt under his shoe, publicly humiliated her to the point where she had tried to take her own life. At the very least she wanted him to remember her for a while when she did the same to him.

She didn't doubt for a minute that anything she said would be almost instantly dismissed from his mind, but if she could say something that rankled, it might stop him treating anyone else so ruthlessly. The rumours and counter-rumours flying round the little Scottish community after the scene at the hotel had made getting over Ronald so much harder for Gaby.

Tamar spent the rest of the afternoon pulling things together with regard to Greenacres, and then catching up with her mountain of paperwork, which had got sadly neglected over the last few weeks as she had raced about like a mad thing chasing the three properties of which Fiona had spoken. But it had been worth it. Oh, yes, it had certainly been worth it.

She stayed at the office long after all the others had gone home, until, at just gone nine, she felt her desk was clearer and she was in control again. The night was a warm one, and the walk from Taylor and Taylor in Fulham to her tiny flat in Chelsea was just what she needed to unwind from the turmoil of the day. She strolled along in the heavy London air, picking up a hot dog— liberally doused with fried onions—on the way, and reflecting that it was only in the big cities where a woman dressed up to the nines in a designer suit and high heels could wander along eating her dinner out of a paper bag without attracting a second glance.

And she loved it; she really did. After that nightmare time at university, to be inconspicuous was all she asked for. Perhaps that was why she had felt Gaby's humiliation and pain so fiercely? she thought now. Having been through a terribly public chastening herself, she knew how it felt. Not that her circumstances had been so awful as poor Gaby's—at least she hadn't got pregnant—but how did you compare being raped to being fooled into sleeping with someone and then losing a baby when you were openly disgraced? Perhaps they were both as bad as each other, really...

Mike Goodfellow. She could picture one of the lecturers at university now in her mind. Tall, good-looking, married with the requisite 2.4 children and career-minded wife, he had really thought he was the bee's knees. And when he'd offered her extra tuition on her English essays she had really thought he meant just that.

The assault had been painful—she'd been a virgin—and degrading, but over mercifully quickly, and when she had decided to go public and report him, despite his threats, she had discovered she hadn't been the first. Three other girls had come forward, and they'd been just the ones still at the university. No one knew how many other girls he had attacked in the past.

Of course the resulting police action and publicity had been tough, and she had certainly learnt who her friends were, if nothing else, but she had been determined not to creep away like a little whipped dog from the moment she had picked herself up off the floor of his room and limped away to get help. He had been so sure she wouldn't report him, so confident in his ruthlessness. Mike Goodfellow. Never had a name been more inapt...

She'd found it difficult to be alone with a man for a long time after that, but friends like Fiona and Richard had been great, and eventually she had gone on a couple of dates—more to prove to herself she could than anything else. But they had been purely platonic, with nothing more than a brief goodnight kiss.

She'd often felt her heart had gone into cold storage on the man front, and it was that, even more than the rape itself, that she couldn't forgive Mike Goodfellow for. He had taken away so much warmth, fun, excitement and just plain ordinary living from her in a few short, but terrifyingly brutal minutes. Even now she would freeze, or experience the odd moment of blind panic, if a man looked at her in a certain way, or touched her when she wasn't aware of them.

He had received a prison sentence, and she understood his wife had left him in the process, but how could he pay for what he had done to her and others? He couldn't, not really...

It's in the past, *it's in the past.* You're not letting him win. It was what she had told herself every day for the last five years, but it helped, and she had determined she would carry on telling herself the same thing until it no longer became necessary.

She took a deep breath now, finishing the last of the

hot dog and throwing the paper away in the convenient red bin that was positioned just outside the entrance to the terraced house in which her flat was situated, before opening the communal front door with her key.

Once inside, she ran up the two flights of stairs to her little idyll at the top of the house, glad to be home. And the quiet oasis she had created for herself in the midst of the bustle of the big metropolis *was* home, in a way her aunt and uncle's house had never been.

She paused after opening the door to her flat, taking a moment to appreciate the light, pretty surroundings and the fact that it was all hers. Her father's foresight in making a clear, concise will after she was born had meant that on reaching the age of twenty-one she had come into a nice, tidy little nest-egg which had been held in trust for her until that date. It wasn't a fortune, but it had meant she could afford to buy her own little home when she left university, furnish it exactly how she wanted, and still have enough left over to purchase an elderly little runabout to get her from A to B when necessary.

She had barely taken a step or two over the threshold when the phone began to ring in her red and gold sitting room, and strangely, just as she lifted the receiver and spoke her name, she knew who it was...

'Tamar?' Jed Cannon's husky voice caused an involuntary curling of her toes. 'I hope you don't mind me calling you at home?'

'How...how did you get the number?' she prevaricated bemusedly. She didn't know if she minded or not, if she were being truthful, she admitted silently to herself.

'Telephone directory,' he said blandly.

'Oh.' She wondered how many T. McKinleys there were in the London area. She'd have to have a look later. 'How can I help you?' she asked carefully.

'My people can get in to do a survey tomorrow morning,' he said without any preamble, 'and I've already checked with Gerald that that's okay.'

Have you indeed? And it's Gerald now, is it? She was beginning to get mad.

'We've discussed a rough price for getting the work done, and Gerald's quite prepared to drop by the required amount. Now—'

'*Mr Cannon*—' how dare he, how *dare* he take over like this? '—you are aware negotiations of this sort should be done through the estate agents?' she asked icily.

'Who says?' he shot back quickly.

'It really isn't done—'

'Tamar, I couldn't give a pig's ear about what is done and what isn't,' he said, with a smooth arrogance that had her telling herself desperately that she had to remember he was the buyer, that this was a huge deal, that she couldn't afford to get on the wrong side of him and blow it. And that was besides her original plan to worm herself into his life and get him interested before she let him know what was what. Which didn't seem quite such a good idea now, somehow.

'I'm working within a limited time-scale, and I haven't got time for pussy-footing about. Right? Now, if you have a problem with that, I'm sorry, but there it is. Although surely the sooner the deal is clinched, the sooner Gerald's happy, I'm happy, and you get your commission. Yes?'

Blow her commission, the arrogant, supercilious, overbearing—

'*Right?*' he repeated coldly.

'Right,' she agreed tightly, her tone saying something quite different. And she *had* decided whether she minded him calling her at home!

'Tamar…' There was what sounded like a long, impatient sigh. 'Please don't be difficult.'

'I'm not being difficult.' Oh, this was getting ridiculous. What was she doing? She couldn't afford to argue with him like this, she cautioned herself sharply, forcing a sweeter note into her voice as she said, 'I'm not, really, Mr Cannon, but negotiations of this sort are what I get paid for, after all.'

'And in the normal run of things I'm sure they are quite invaluable,' he said soothingly.

'Yes.' Patronising into the bargain, she thought exasperatedly. But at the moment all the cards were stacked well and truly on his side, and all she could do was grit her teeth and play ball. 'Well, if Mr Biggsley-Brown is happy with what you've discussed, I'm sure we will be,' she said brightly. 'I'll have to ring him in the morning and confirm, of course.'

'Of course,' he agreed drily. 'But I'm sure you'll find he's very understanding.'

Huh! She narrowed her eyes, frowning across the room. And what was all the mad rush about anyway? Why was it so imperative for him to have a house so quickly? He had a marvellous bachelor pad—a sumptuous penthouse from all accounts—in Kensington. It wasn't as though he didn't have anywhere of his own to live.

He was just being awkward—flexing his wealthy muscles and demanding that everything be done yesterday, because that was how *he* wanted it. Ruthless to the last, she thought bitterly.

'Yes... Well, thank you for letting me know what you've done, and I'll be in touch once—'

'Are you free for dinner tomorrow night?' Jed interrupted evenly.

'Dinner?'

Eager delight was quite absent from her voice, and his own reflected his recognition of the fact when he said, his tone smooth but distinctly cool, 'It's something most people do in between lunch one day and breakfast the next.'

Dinner. Tamar was eternally grateful Jed Cannon couldn't see her as she leant back against the wall and shut her eyes for a moment, before taking a deep steadying breath and saying, the breathless note not at all feigned, 'I'm so sorry, but I do have a previous engagement tomorrow...' in the sort of voice which made it clear she would like him to suggest another evening when she could make it.

He did. 'Wednesday evening?' he asked expressionlessly.

Wednesday. That would give her Tuesday lunchtime and evening, and Wednesday lunchtime if she needed it, to buy a new outfit, have her hair done, give herself a beauty treatment... 'That would be lovely,' she said quietly, hoping she was hitting the right note of cool interest now.

'Good. I'll pick you up about eight,' he said smoothly. 'I was thinking we might go to Harvey's, unless you have any objection?'

Tamar just stopped herself saying, Harvey's? in the

same blank, gormless way she had said, Dinner?, and instead managed to sound quite blasé when she answered, 'No, Harvey's will be fine.'

Harvey's will be fine. After she had said goodbye and put the phone down she had a sudden desire to laugh hysterically. Harvey's was the one nightclub in London that even the rich and famous would kill to get membership for, and there wasn't one single person of her acquaintance who had got so much as a nose in the door. And he was taking her there! Her, Tamar McKinley!

The urge to laugh vanished instantly as the thought of what she was going to wear surfaced with frightening intent. You couldn't go to Harvey's in an off-the-peg dress and shoes, she thought with blind panic. This was going to be an exclusive designer job at the very least. Well, she would have to use the money in her building society account that she had been saving all year for a holiday, and maybe the cash she had put by for her car too. Needs must.

She went straight into her tiny but extremely well fitted kitchen and made herself a very strong cup of black coffee, which she drank down scalding hot in an effort to combat her churning stomach. It helped, and after she had drunk a second cup her natural optimism and determination came to the fore.

Jed Cannon was just a man, when all was said and done. All right, he might be wealthier and better-looking than most, and have enough charisma and male magnetism to send the average woman bandy, but *she* wasn't the average woman. She made a deep obeisance with her head to the thought. And he was going to remember her—and Gaby by the time she had finished—for a long, long time.

CHAPTER THREE

TAMAR knew, when she looked into Jed Cannon's silver-grey gaze and saw it narrow to laser-like intentness the moment before he smiled, that the short jade-green silk cocktail dress, with its wafer-thin straps and simple crossover style bodice, had been worth every penny. And the matching shoes, with their high, high heels and neat little ankle straps, were just right too, emphasising her long legs and slim shape perfectly.

The price had been astronomical, but it had been the way the outfit showed off her figure that had made her hesitate in purchasing it at first. Since Mike Goodfellow's attack, she had been chary about wearing anything too revealing, hiding in big baggy tops and jeans the first year, before slowly graduating to more tailored feminine clothes as time had gone on—but always with a view to modesty and propriety.

But you didn't go to somewhere like Harvey's muffled up to the ears. Even she knew that. And so...

'You look very lovely, Tamar.'

She wondered if the sexy huskiness as his deep voice lingered over her name was a well-tried and proved strategy? Whatever, it was very effective. But she was immune to his charm. *She was.*

'Thank you.' She smiled brightly. He looked absolutely wonderful, but she wasn't going to tell him so. The light cream dinner jacket sat on the big male shoulders in a way that proclaimed the wearer was used to such formal wear, and there was an easy grace about him that suggested restrained animal power. He was a sensual man... The thought shocked her into stepping out of the hall and into the street beyond as she said, 'Shall we go?' in as neutral a voice as she could manage.

She had been ready and waiting in the hall for his knock for over fifteen minutes, determined he wasn't going to set foot inside the house. She didn't want him in the place, and most certainly not in her flat, although she couldn't quite have explained why. She had tried to tell herself it was because she needed to keep all this on her terms, but it wasn't that, not really. She just didn't want him getting...close.

'Do I make you nervous, Tamar?'

He had ushered her into the cab with gentle decorum, making polite small talk for some moments, so now, as he twisted to face her, the silver eyes hard on her flushed face, he didn't miss the start she gave at his softly voiced question.

'Nervous? Of course not!' She forced a light laugh, and then coughed as it strangled in her throat.

'Good...' He didn't sound as though he believed her, and his next words added weight to this impression when he said, still in the same quiet, soft tone, 'You don't want to believe everything you hear, you know. One of the disadvantages of a high profile is that rumours abound on all fronts, whether personal or workwise. If I had done or said all the things accredited to me I'd have burnt myself out long ago.'

'And you're not burnt out,' she stated with provocative primness, almost as though she disapproved.

He wanted to laugh, but managed to restrain the impulse, knowing it would not be appreciated. She intrigued him, this serious dark-eyed flame-haired beauty; she intrigued him very much. There was something about her he couldn't fathom, and it made a pleasant change from most of the women he knew, who were veritable open books.

'No, I'm not burnt out, Tamar,' he agreed with straight-faced control, and then, as she nodded solemnly before dropping her eyes and moistening her lips with a small pink tongue, he felt his breath quicken and a stirring in his loins.

It was that, the almost tangible innocence about her, he told himself with self-deprecating mockery, that got him. She was full of little gestures like that, but he'd bet his life she wasn't aware of the effect they had on the average male. But she must be, he told himself in the next instant. Of course she must be. You didn't get to her age, looking like she did, without knowing a thing or two. She was just more subtle than most; that was all. But he liked it. He had to admit he liked it.

Harvey's was nowhere as big as Tamar had expected it to be, but in every other respect it came up to expectation. The small tables clustered around the dance floor were shadowed and intimate, the food was superb, and the frothy pink cocktails followed by a bottle of champagne that gave a new meaning to the phrase 'nectar of the gods' were out of this world.

It was clearly a place to see and be seen, and, judging by the number of people who tried to catch Jed Cannon's eye, Tamar assumed he had more than a little influence. And didn't he just love it? Tamar thought to herself, as the head waiter glided over to their table for the umpteenth time to check if everything was all right. The

ostentation, the peacock-like display of all those present—he took it all in through those narrowed silver eyes
without betraying a single thought or emotion. An ice
man. She gave a mental nod to the thought. Definitely
a control freak…

And then the tasteful little floor show ended, just as
Tamar finished the most delicious liqueur coffee of her
life, and Jed rose slowly, his eyes slumberous as he said,
'Dance with me, Tamar?'

Dance with him? She stared up at him, her eyes wide.
Of course she should have expected this, prepared herself for it, but foolishly she had been so taken up with
the spectacle of it all that she hadn't thought about dancing with him.

He looked very big and very dark, the pale cream of
his dinner jacket emphasising the threatening enigmatic
maleness, and she suddenly felt she had caught a tiger
by the tail. She must be mad—stark, staring mad—to
think she could influence Jed Cannon by the tiniest
amount. He was a man who used women for his own
purposes, it was written all over him, and she was way,
way out of her league here.

'Tamar?' He held out his hand, and she could do nothing else but rise and take it, her stomach quivering as
his warm flesh made contact with hers.

Once on the dance floor a new realisation of his big-
ness swept over her as he took her into his arms, and
she had to steel herself not to panic. This was the first
time in years—since Mike Goodfellow's attack, in
fact—that she had consciously allowed a man to hold
her in this way. The thought did nothing to help the little
shivers flickering down her spine as the subtle but delicious smell of him encompassed her.

And then her chin rose a notch and her mouth tight-ened resolutely. She could do this, she could, and if she could handle being in Jed Cannon's arms, she could han-dle being in anyone's. There was nothing like starting at the top and working down...

'Relax.' His voice was deep and quiet above her head as he nestled the soft, cloudy curls with his chin and pulled her a little closer. 'I don't know what stories you've heard about the big, bad wolf, but I'm not going to eat you. You're quite safe.'

'I know.'

Her voice wasn't as steady as she would have liked it to be, and then, as he chuckled low in his throat and said, 'Now that's not a very nice thing to say. I must be slipping,' she took a long, hard, silent breath and prayed for control.

This was just social intercourse, flirting, part of a date. That was all. She knew it, in her head, but she was so out of practice in this realm that every little word or gesture he made was intimidating.

And then she felt him move slightly, and he pulled away enough to lift her chin with one hand as he stared down into her huge velvet-brown eyes. 'You're enchant-ing, do you know that?' he murmured softly. 'A lady of contrasts.'

'Contrasts?' She dared not relax into the sensual in-timate mood he was creating—this had to move along slowly, very slowly. No doubt he was used to women falling into bed with him at the drop of a hat, and in the sophisticated worldly circles in which he moved affairs were conducted with a swiftness that could take your breath away, she thought silently. But this time, *this* time he wasn't going to have it all his own way. 'I don't think so.'

'But, yes.' The husky voice did something to her nerve-endings that was undescribable. 'I've seen the smart, efficient career woman, totally sure of herself and her ability to deliver the goods, the sophisticated beauty who has dazzled and bewitched every man in the place, and then there's the other Tamar, the gentle, innocent, shy little girl...'

It hurt. The 'innocent' hurt—which was ridiculous really, when she had thought she'd got over Mike Goodfellow stealing what should have been hers to give long ago.

'"Gentle, innocent, shy little girl"?' She smiled as she said it, and he would never know how much self-discipline it took. 'In London?'

But he had seen the brown darken to ebony, and the impact of his words in the dark depths. 'Why not?' he countered easily. 'They tell me the age of miracles is not yet passed.'

And then he drew her close again, and she had to concentrate all her efforts on staying upright as the feel and smell of him caused her legs to turn to jelly. She tried to tell herself it was nerves that was sending tiny electric shocks all over her body, but she knew, even before he bent his head and took her lips in the lightest of kisses, that it wasn't that.

She was attracted to him. The shock of self-awareness along with the feel of his warm, firm lips on hers stunned her for a moment, and he had raised his head again, continuing to move easily around the small dance floor, weaving in and out of the other couples who had joined them, before she regained her senses.

Oh, no, she didn't want to be attracted to Jed Cannon—he was the last man in the world she wanted to feel anything for, albeit a purely physical desire of the flesh.

Her mind continued to scream a warning all the time she was in his arms, and she was heartily glad when the music finished and he led her back to their table, one hand in the small of her back.

'So...' He smiled at her once they were seated. 'Tell me a bit about yourself,' he said softly.

Oh, help. The beautiful wild silk dress, the incredibly expensive tousled sexy hairdo and carefully applied make-up didn't seem much protection against that laser-sharp gaze when it hit head-on.

'Me?' she squeaked weakly. 'There's not anything to tell.'

'I don't believe you.'

It wasn't so much what he said as the way he said it that caused the alarm bells to go off, and her eyes widened for a moment before she forced a smile and said, 'Well, if you don't mind a boring thirty seconds...?'

'Try me,' he said evenly, his eyes tight on her face.

'Born twenty-four years ago, parents died when I was a child, lived with my aunt and uncle and cousins before going to university and then getting my present job.' She smiled brightly. 'That's it.'

The hell that was it. The more he knew about her the less he knew, Jed Cannon thought darkly. And the way she had trembled in his arms on that dance floor...

'You were wrong. It wasn't boring, and it only lasted ten seconds,' he said easily. 'So, where did you live as a child? Here in London?'

'No.' She didn't really want to say, but there was no

way she could avoid it without making him suspicious.
'Scotland, actually.'

'With your father's kin?' he pressed gently.

'His sister—my aunt Prudence.'

'Right.' He nodded slowly. 'Beautiful place to spend
your childhood. I had some business interests in that
neck of the woods a while back, as it happens, although
I didn't get up there much.'

No, you just sent that slimeball of a brother-in-law of
yours, Tamar thought grimly as she smiled and said,
'Really?'

'Yes, near Inverness. A little company we bought and
then sold on.'

Oh, yes, she knew all about him selling it on—it
hadn't been just Gaby who had lost her job in the
merger, but half the workforce. Not that Gaby had cared
about her job at that point; she had been too devastated
by Ronald Mitchell's betrayal and the loss of her baby.
Her cousin hadn't had a clue that the young, dynamic
handsome troubleshooter was married, and he had
played her like a master violinist until she was putty in
his hands.

'Sold on?' Tamar looked straight at him and tried for
an artlessly ingenuous tone as she said, 'Don't people
lose their jobs when that happens?'

'Not always.' The silver eyes had sharpened somewhat, so perhaps the open, simple approach hadn't
worked. 'And we try to minimise redundancies wherever
we can.'

His tone was slightly irritable—he clearly didn't like
the way the conversation was going, Tamar thought with
some satisfaction. As a seduction technique it wasn't a
winner...

'I see.' She kept her voice guileless. 'That must be a comfort to people.'

'Yes.' It was abrupt.

The piercing gaze was trying to dissect her mind. He clearly wasn't at all sure where she was coming from and whether to take her words at face value, Tamar thought delightedly, relishing the moment. She decided not to push her luck any further, contenting herself with, 'I'm sure it's a very heavy responsibility for you,' before she said, 'And you? What about you?'

'I'm sure I couldn't tell you anything more than you know already,' he said coolly, with a lift of dark, sardonic eyebrows. 'One thing I have come to realise is that you do your homework very thoroughly.'

Touché, Mr Cannon. 'Thank you.' She smiled sweetly. 'I try to be as conscientious as time and resources permit.'

Something had shifted in the last few minutes, and he wasn't sure what it was. He stared at her, his eyes searching and his mouth straight. But one thing was for sure; what you saw was not what you got with Miss Tamar McKinley. And now, added to the intrigue he felt about this woman, he recognised excitement too, and it had been a long, long time since that particular emotion had stirred his mind and body...

They left Harvey's at gone one in the morning, and Tamar didn't want to acknowledge that she had enjoyed herself immensely, but she had. Since their conversation about Scotland nothing faintly personal had been discussed, Jed putting himself out to be an entertaining, amusing and very witty dinner companion, with a darkly wicked line in humour that exactly matched her own.

And more disturbing still, if she had reflected on it,

was the fact that for most of the evening she had completely forgotten her purpose in accepting a date with Jed Cannon. Gaby and Ronald and all that side of things had been a million miles from her thoughts.

But it all resurfaced as they stepped out of the flamboyantly unreal world of the nightclub into the warm, traffic-scented London night, and Jed took her arm as he said, his voice soft and husky, 'Fancy a nightcap at my place?'

'I don't think so.'

The taxi was waiting, and as he opened her door and she slid into the leather-clad interior, he added, 'I do mean just a nightcap, Tamar, in case you were wondering.'

Oh, yes, and pigs might fly. 'I'm sure you do,' she lied carefully, forcing herself not to show any reaction as he joined her on the back seat, his thigh against hers and his arm loosely round the back of the seat, half resting against her shoulders. 'But I've got to get up for work in the morning.'

'Home it is, then.' Perversely she felt quite peeved at his easy acceptance of her refusal, her eyes on his dark profile as he leant forward in the seat to give the taxi driver her address. She was close enough to see the dark, budding growth of his beard underneath the firm, tanned skin of his face, the way his chiselled cheekbones emphasised the strength of his mouth and his very male square chin. It was a sexy mouth...

As he relaxed back in the seat again she jerked her mind back from such dangerous thoughts, but could do nothing to stop the hot colour flooding up under her skin. She didn't want to be attracted to Jed Cannon, in fact he was the very last man in the world she wanted to feel anything for, but he seemed to have provoked a whole host of confusing emotions she hadn't been aware of until this moment.

He frightened her. She wrestled with the thought for a moment or two, unwilling to give it credence, but then submitted to the truth. Yes, he did. He frightened her. But not in the normal sort of way. It was more as if she was frightened of herself when she was with him...

Oh, don't be so plain *stupid*, she told herself angrily as the taxi drew away from the kerb and Jed turned to her, very much the smooth, assured man about town as he made some casual remark about the evening. He's just your average common or garden rat, that's all. Don't give him powers he doesn't possess.

Nevertheless, she was vitally aware of the big male body next to her as the taxi sped across town, the latent power in the muscled frame and the alien smell and feel of him intrusive, and such was her relief when the taxi drew up outside the big old terraced house in which her flat was housed, that she was out of the car before he had had time to come round and open her door.

She saw one dark eyebrow quirk, heard him say something she couldn't quite catch to the taxidriver, and then he had walked round to join her on the pavement.

'Thank you for a lovely evening,' she said, a little too quickly. 'I'll be in touch about Mr Biggsley-Brown's survey and—'

'Tamar, I always see my dates home,' he said evenly.

'I am home.' She stared up into the dark, expressionless face in surprise.

'It's nearly half past one in the morning; I would prefer to see you to your door,' he said coolly.

'There's no need, really.' She smiled brightly, but it

was water off a duck's back, and the handsome, cold face didn't alter expression by so much as the blink of an eyelid. Oh, wonderful, absolutely one hundred per cent wonderful, Tamar thought testily. He was clearly going to make an issue of this, and what with the late hour, and the taxi purring away gently in the background, she really didn't feel like a head-on confrontation.

She stared at him for a moment more before conceding defeat. At least he'd got the message that she wasn't in the running for a quick tumble between the sheets anyway, she reassured herself silently. She couldn't have made that any clearer. But, Gaby or no Gaby, she wouldn't have another date with him—if he asked her to, that was. This whole thing had been a crazy idea and she wished, oh, she so *wished* she'd never started it.

Once the sale of the house had gone through she would make an appointment to see him and tell him exactly what she thought of him. She would love to do it now, but it wasn't fair on Fiona and Richard to blow such a huge contract and be totally unprofessional into the bargain.

'Tamar?'

She realised she was still staring at him somewhat vacantly and flushed slightly, her voice defensive when she said, 'I...I'd better open the door,' and turned towards the house.

She could feel him right behind her as she fumbled with the key, and, ridiculous though she knew it was, it panicked her; the memory of how it had been with Mike Goodfellow—her innate helplessness beneath his male strength, his brutality, his overwhelming sexual desire— suddenly flaring into life.

Once inside the dark hall, she switched on the light quickly, and then hid her hands behind her back as she realised they were trembling. 'My…my flat is at the top of the house. I'll be perfectly all right now…'

'I'm sure you will, but I prefer to make sure,' he said reasonably.

She nodded, masking her nervousness under a light laugh as she said, 'Don't tell me—you're the sort of man who sees old grannies across the road and gives up his seat for a lady?'

'A dying breed,' he agreed with a smile. Dammit, she was like a cat on a hot tin roof. What the hell had she heard about him to make her like this?

He followed her up the two flights of stairs slowly, and by the time they reached the top floor of the house he admitted to himself that he was angry. She made him feel like some sort of sexual pervert, he thought grimly, and he didn't like it one little bit. Her hands had been shaking when she'd tried to open that damn door; he'd seen them. Did she really think he was so desperate for a woman that he would take one against her will? Was that it?

His thoughts made his voice curt as Tamar paused outside the front door of the flat. 'Right, have a look inside and make sure everything is all right and I'll be off.'

She scuttled inside like a frightened rabbit, reappearing a few moments later to say, 'Everything's fine,' her eyes huge and dark in the dim light from the one solitary lightbulb on the narrow landing, and her red-gold hair glowing softly like a banked-down fire.

He had intended, after the last few minutes, to leave without touching her again, so now, as he suddenly stepped forward and took her in his arms, he was as surprised as she was.

Before she could really grasp what was happening, his dark head had bent to hers and his mouth had taken hers in a delicate, tantalising kiss that was warm and unhurried and very, very pleasurable. For one moment she could sense his restrained power, the breadth and height of his big body, the smell of his skin and the dark force of his maleness, and she was aware she was enjoying being in his arms, wanting more—and then he stepped away from her, his voice cool as he said, 'Goodnight, Tamar. Sleep well.'

Sleep well? She watched, stunned, as he turned, without another word or a backward glance, and disappeared down the stairs.

He had gone? Just like that? She continued standing at the open door until the sound of the taxi drawing away in the street outside jolted her out of her daze, and then she turned quickly, entering the flat and closing the door with an irritable gesture that almost made the door bang.

How could she have let him kiss her like that? How could she have *enjoyed* it, more to the point? She knew what he was like, for goodness' sake. Besides all the trauma about Gaby, her research had shown that he had a different woman for every day of the week, and that none of them lasted above a few months or so. He was a philanderer, a typical millionaire-playboy-type, although in his case he worked hard *and* played hard, rather than just the latter.

She shut her eyes tightly, leaning against the closed door and touching her lips with a tentative hand as they continued to tingle with the memory of the sensually soft kiss. *She hadn't been frightened or repulsed by his em-*

brace. The relief she would have felt at such self-awareness over any other man was completely missing. In fact—and now her eyes snapped open and she groaned softly—she would have liked the kiss to continue, would have liked to snuggle closer into that male-scented body and have him *really* kiss her.

No, no, she wouldn't. She bounced her head sharply in agreement to the declaration, her mouth thinning and her body straightening. Jed Cannon was the enemy, however he had tried to appear tonight. And, apart from that one last meeting she had promised herself, she was going to have nothing more to do with him.

There was a lot more to Miss Tamar McKinley than met the eye. Jed Cannon's face was thoughtful as he slid back into the taxi after giving the address of his apartment in Kensington to the driver. He had sensed that earlier in the evening at Harvey's, and now the sensation that she was hiding something came back even more strongly, vying with the intense surge of sexual desire that still had him as hard as a rock.

How long had it been since a woman had affected him like this one? Years…over a decade in fact. His mind touched on Jennie, but the memory of her had long since ceased to hold any power to hurt. He had been wild for a time after she had let him down so badly, indulging in one one-night stand after another, until the shock of his father's death had sobered him up a little. The steadying process had been completed when his mother had died and Emma had become so ill—and he had found out the dark secret his mother had thought she had taken to her grave…

He made a physical movement with his body to dismiss the blackness reflections on that time always induced, his handsome face hardening before it settled into the chilling mask of cold imperturbability with which he normally faced the world.

He didn't know if it was wise to see Tamar McKinley again, but he would. He shut his eyes, leaning back against the seat for all the world as if he was dozing, although sleep was the last thing on his mind. He had had a taste of her now, and he wanted more, much more.

She wasn't the type he normally went for, this willo'-the-wisp Titian-haired beauty, who was such an engaging mixture of brash career woman and shy, elusive innocent, but that didn't matter.

Of course, the image she projected was a carefully nurtured one, no doubt—on all counts. He sighed cynically. And about as real as Santa Claus in this dog-eatdog world. But it was alluring, beguiling—as it was meant to be.

Yes, he was going to enjoy finding out who and what the real Tamar McKinley was...

CHAPTER FOUR

TAMAR grimaced to herself as she ran up the stairs to the flat, where she could hear her telephone ringing with offensive perseverance. The day had been the epitome of every worst Monday rolled into one, with two clients pulling out of sales at the last moment, irate customers taking out their frustration on her, both Fiona and Richard down with a virulent summer flu that threatened to keep them away from the office all week, and Tim depressed and morose after being dumped by his latest girlfriend. And then, as the icing on the cake, she had got caught in a sudden September cloudburst on the way home and had squelched the last few hundred yards to the house soaked through to the skin.

She was cold, wet, exhausted and hungry, she told herself as she opened the front door and kicked off her shoes before diving for the phone, and she didn't want to talk to anyone. A long, hot bath with a glass of sherry at the side of her before a quick convenience meal in front of the TV, courtesy of the microwave, was all she asked of life right at this moment.

'Hallo?' She couldn't keep the irritation out of her voice as she spoke into the receiver.

'Hallo, Tamar.' There was only one deep, gravelly voice in the world which could speak her name like that, and she sat down very suddenly in a dripping heap on the carpet.

Jed Cannon? Now why was he phoning her? He had

phoned twice in the week following their dinner date. Each time she had refused his invitation to the theatre and a meal, and she hadn't heard from him in the last three weeks. The sale had gone through successfully, and with no hiccups, and as far as she knew he had moved into Greenacres a few days ago—at which point she had determined she would make an appointment to see him as soon as possible to tell him exactly what she thought of him. But then Fiona and Richard had succumbed to the dreaded bug and her life, hectic and chaotic at the best of times, had seemed to go mad.

'This is Jed Cannon.' The dark voice was silky-soft. 'I trust I haven't caught you at an inconvenient moment?'

Well, she didn't have to be polite or tactful any more. 'Actually, you have.' She paused before saying tightly, 'I've just got in from work, as it happens.'

'You work too hard.'

It wasn't meant as a compliment, and she frowned at the telephone before saying stiffly, 'I disagree.'

'Naturally.' His voice was even and cool, and irritated her more than words could say. 'But it is almost nine o'clock, and I dare say you were in the office before nine this morning? Twelve-hour working days were abolished years ago, along with sending small boys up chimneys and slave labour, or did no one bother to tell you?'

'Fiona and Richard are ill; I'm holding the fort,' she snapped brusquely.

'And when they aren't ill?' he asked smoothly.

'Look...' She wasn't going to win this one if she spoke the truth, so it was better to change the subject now. 'What is it you've phoned about? Is anything wrong?'

'Does there have to be something wrong for me to phone you, Tamar?' he asked softly, and then, 'I'm ringing with an invitation. I'm holding a little housewarming party at the weekend, and I would like you to come. You did find the house for me, after all.'

'It's my job,' she said quickly.

'I'd still like to say thank you.'

What should she do? Tamar bit back the initial response that sprang to her lips and took a long deep breath as she tried to consider her next words. She still fully intended to have her say over Gaby, so perhaps this opportunity was better than making a formal appointment? She'd stirred his interest—this third call asking to see her proved that—and she hadn't changed her mind about steering clear of this man. He was...dangerous. So, all things being equal, might this be just the time to have everything brought out into the open and have done with it?

'You don't really need to say thank you, but it's very kind of you to invite me, and, yes, I'd love to come.' She heard herself say the words with a sudden feeling of impending doom.

'Good.' Just one little word—so why did his voice make her shiver as it caught at the hitherto unawakened sensual side of her psyche? 'Saturday evening, seven o'clock. I'll send a car for you.'

'There's no need—'

He cut off her hasty reply as he repeated steadily, 'My chauffeur will be outside your flat at seven, Tamar,' before he replaced the receiver and the phone went dead.

She didn't *want* his car to come for her— especially

in view of what she intended to say and the inevitable consequences. Tamar glared at the innocent plastic, her brow furrowed. But that was typical of Jed Cannon, wasn't it? Bulldozing his way through people's lives, Mr Macho Man...

She wriggled irritably, and then, as the sogginess of her clothes and her still dripping hair made itself felt, sighed loudly. Let him have it his way. After Saturday night she wasn't going to see him again, so it didn't much matter one way or the other.

Strangely, the thought dampened her still further, and she jumped briskly to her feet after one more moment of brooding contemplation, saying out loud, 'Saturday night and then that *will* be the end of all this,' as though someone had argued the point with her. And even when she was ensconced in the steaming bubbles a few minutes later, with a large glass of sherry in one hand and her head resting on her bath cushion, she found she was still altercating with the inner voice that had challenged the sincerity of her wanting Jed Cannon out of her orbit for good.

Tamar slept in late on Saturday morning, and woke to a mild, balmy September day that was completely at odds with the fury of the wind and stormy rain of the previous days. She stretched slowly in the warmth of her snug little bed, curling her toes and luxuriating in her first Saturday away from the office for months.

Fiona and Richard had struggled back to their little empire on Thursday morning, both looking like death but equally determined that the business would fall apart if they were away one more day. In spite of their fragile condition, they had insisted Tamar take a long overdue Saturday off once they heard of Jed's invitation.

'I can't believe the amount of work you've got through this week,' Fiona had exclaimed gratefully when she had viewed her and Richard's virtually empty desktops. 'You must have camped out here.'

'Almost.' Tamar had grinned wryly.

'Then you pamper yourself on Saturday,' Fiona had continued, in rare motherly mode. 'Lie in, give yourself a beauty treatment, veg out...'

Veg out. Tamar looked up at the ceiling as she reflected ruefully that it would take a stronger will than hers to relax enough to 'veg out', knowing that in a few hours it was to cross swords with Jed Cannon. Now she was awake she found her mind was buzzing. Nevertheless, she forced herself to lie in bed for another thirty minutes before realising the ridiculousness of her actions. Once up, she pulled on an old jumper and jeans and cleaned the flat from top to bottom. It took three hours, but at the end of that time every surface and nook and cranny was bright and sparkling, and a good deal of nervous energy had been burnt up in the process.

Disciplining her mind and body was something she had learnt in the aftermath of the assault. It had been a straight choice between hard physical labour—which in those days had meant a punishing regime of jogging and squash in between lectures and working at her books— or a visit to the doctor for drugs to help her sleep and eat and keep a tentative hold on her sanity. She had chosen the exercise. And it had worked...in a way. Enough to keep her reasonably level-headed most of the time anyway, she thought now as she surveyed the gleaming flat. And—in spite of it being the most over-worked cliché ever—time *was* a great healer.

For every Mike Goodfellow and Jed Cannon there were a hundred kind, decent, generous folk. She switched on the coffee machine and watched it as it began to gurgle and splutter, but the feeling that she had been less than generous in linking the two men together nagged at her conscience, and she clicked on the radio to take her mind off her thoughts as she made herself a quick lunch of salad and cold meat.

By half past six that evening she was ready and wait-ing for Jed's chauffeur, and as nervous as a kitten. But she looked good, she told herself reassuringly as she glanced in the tall, narrow mirror in her small bedroom one last time, before walking through to the sitting room.

Her mid-calf-length skirt and short-sleeved top in soft, voluptuous white cashmere were just right for a cool September evening, and although not new, or a designer exclusive, they were both chic and elegant. She wore the minimum of jewellery—simple pearl studs in her ears and a thin gold bracelet which had been her mother's in the shape of tiny daisies, on her left wrist—and she wore her hair up in a thick loose knot on the top of her head, with an odd curl here and there about her face and neck to soften the look. Her eyes, aided and abetted by dusky grey eyeshadow and black mascara, looked enormous, her skin was flawless and her full, pouting mouth was shown off to perfection by the flaming red lipstick she had bought the day before.

She fully intended to exit from Jed Cannon's life with a bang.

That resolve stayed with her all the way to Jed's house as she sat in splendid isolation in the back of the chauffeur-driven Mercedes, and, although faltering slightly at the sight of the crowd of prestige cars in the drive of Greenacres, only finally evaporated on her entrance into the house.

The place was swarming, quite literally swarming, with the beautiful people—gold and diamonds flashing on every wrist and at every throat of the females present, and the men debonair, cool and distinguished in their exquisitely cut dinner jackets and bow ties. It was like a scene from an elaborate Hollywood movie, and Tamar had never felt so out of place anywhere in her life.

'Tamar.' She had no time to reflect further, as the deep, dark voice at her elbow told her Jed must have been looking out for her.

'Hallo.' She swung round with a bright smile on her face and then froze at the sight of him. He looked gorgeous, far, far too gorgeous, and suddenly she was terrifyingly vulnerable. She hadn't expected the animal panic and exposed defencelessness which ripped through her as the beautiful silver eyes smiled down at her, but they were there, and they showed on her face. As his smile began to die, she forced herself to say something, anything, to defuse what had become an unbearably charged moment. 'The…the house looks wonderful. But didn't you say a little party?' she asked, as lightly as she could manage. 'There must be over a hundred people here.'

'Hundred and fifty,' he admitted quietly, taking her arm as he continued, 'I'll introduce you to a few folk.'

Tamar could never remember much about the next hour or so as she and Jed moved from one group to another; all she was conscious of was the feel of his warm hand in the small of her back as he guided her about the vast house, and the way he kept her at his side.

How could you be so helplessly attracted to someone you loathed? she asked herself over and over again, as she smiled and nodded and said all the right things at the right time. It was so *stupid*. She didn't want to fancy him, and he wasn't at all the sort of man she had been attracted to in the past.

Her preference had always veered towards males with boyish good looks, rather than he-man types, and the faintly Nordic, fair-haired male had appealed. Jed Cannon was neither boyish nor fair-haired, and the only thing Nordic about him was his fierce aggressive nature which was pure Viking.

At eight-thirty, one of the uniformed caterers informed the guests a hot and cold buffet was being served in the dining room. As people began to wind their way towards that room Jed steered her into a quiet corner and bent down to whisper in her ear, 'If you could only relax a little, you might find you actually begin to enjoy this evening, Tamar.'

'What?' She blinked up at him, sure she must have misheard his words in the general furore towards the dining room.

His mouth twisted, and black brows rose over mocking silver eyes as he smiled down at her. 'You're like a cat on a hot tin roof,' he said smoothly, 'and you know it.'

'I am not.' But dark colour had flared over her cheekbones and they both knew she was lying.

'Tamar, you have one hundred and fifty chaperons; what more do you want?' he asked evenly.

One thousand and fifty would be no good if Jed

Cannon wanted a woman, she thought helplessly, a little curl of something hot pulsing in her lower stomach. She was excited, sexually excited, she realised, with a little shock of horror, *over Jed Cannon*. Oh, this was ridiculous, *she* was ridiculous, and she was going to tell him all right now. That he had been set up from the start, that she despised and hated him, and why. And then she would leave, go and find a taxi somewhere, and put the last month or so behind her.

'I'll tell you what I want, shall I?' she challenged tightly, stepping back a pace away from his body.

His eyes had narrowed at the look on her face, and his voice held a faint note of perplexity as he said, 'Why don't you do just that, Tamar?'

And her mouth was already open, the words hovering on her lips, when a quiet voice at the side of them said, 'Jed? You haven't introduced us, but this can only be Tamar.'

Looking back on it later, Tamar would acknowledge that it was only the years of training in hiding her thoughts and emotions after the rape that allowed her to smile down at the young woman in the wheelchair and say in a perfectly normal voice, 'Yes, I'm Tamar, but you seem to have the advantage over me.'

'Emma...Cannon.' The slight pause before the surname was awkward, but as Tamar shook the proffered hand she kept her face bland and smiling.

'My sister, Emma. Emma, this is Tamar, as you so rightly deduced. There, official introductions over—all right?' Jed was teasing his sister indulgently, but Tamar saw a wealth of love in the dark, hard face as he looked down at the slight young woman in the wheelchair, and it both amazed and pained her. And why was Emma in the chair anyway, and using her maiden name again? Tamar asked herself bewilderedly. What was going on, and where was her rat of a husband?

'I'm sorry I'm late coming down, but...' Emma's voice dwindled away, but Jed seemed to understand her unspoken explanation anyway.

He patted her hand and said, 'You're doing fine, just fine,' before turning to Tamar and adding, 'She looks beautiful, doesn't she?'

Tamar nodded, her eyes soft as she smiled at Emma, who had gone brick-red at her brother's words. 'I gather he's the devoted big brother, right?' she asked lightly, with a little wink at the other girl. 'And I bet he bashed anyone who pulled your pigtails when you were kids too.'

'He did.' Emma was laughing now. 'Frequently. He was always coming home with a bloody nose or cut lip.'

'Hang on, hang on, you'll have her believing I was some sort of ruffian,' Jed protested with mock sternness, but Tamar had noticed how his face had relaxed when Emma had smiled.

He's concerned about her. In fact he's worried to death, Tamar thought with an intuition she hadn't known she had. The knowledge pulled at her heartstrings in a way she could well have done without. She didn't want Jed Cannon to show any normal human softness or gentleness; she couldn't afford him to. She had to keep the picture she had painted of him after his ruthlessness with Gaby clear in her mind.

The three of them talked for a few minutes, Jed and Emma chaffing each other much as she and Gaby might have done, Tamar noticed unwillingly, and then, as a serious young man with earnest brown eyes and over-long hair came up to talk to Emma, Jed tactfully drew Tamar away.

'That's the man she should have married,' he stated with surprising directness.

'What?' Tamar stopped stock-still and stared at him, open-mouthed. He looked back at her, totally unabashed.

'They've been friends since school days, but he left it too late to declare his feelings,' Jed said calmly. 'And in the mean time a certain Mr Ronald Mitchell appeared on the scene and swept her off her feet with empty promises and a glib tongue.'

'Ronald...?' Tamar prevaricated weakly, finding herself left quite out of her depth by the sudden turn events had taken.

'Her husband—soon to be ex-husband,' Jed said grimly. 'And I won't offend your ears by telling you the names I have for him privately. He latched on to Emma because he saw her as an easy meal ticket, nothing more, and he was unfaithful from the first month of their marriage.' He suddenly seemed to realise he had said more than he intended, and waved a hand dismissively as he finished, 'But that's history.'

Tamar glanced over her shoulder, to where Emma and the young man were deep in conversation, and then back to Jed as she said, 'She's not well?'

It was a rhetorical question, and he treated it as such. 'Degenerative bone disease,' he said shortly, his voice expressionless, with the sort of control that hides crucifying pain.

'Oh, I'm so sorry,' she murmured shakily.

'She's been under treatment with a doctor in the States for almost two years now,' Jed said quietly. 'He wanted to try a new pioneer treatment—Emma is something of a guinea pig, I guess— but the alternative...' He shrugged grimly.

'Anyway, her husband recently conducted such a flagrant affair that even Emma couldn't ignore it, especially when she returned home a day early from the States and found them in the marital bed.' Tamar concealed a sigh of relief. For an awful moment she had thought he was talking about Gaby and Ronald. 'So she's living with me for the time being. That's why I was in such a rush to get the house ready,' he added quietly. 'She has to have a week's treatment in the States every month, and I wanted a stable base here in England for her. My apartment's no good—a typical bachelor pad,' he finished wryly. 'Here she has the garden and the pool, and swimming is very good for her condition.'

'Right.' Tamar nodded slowly, her head whirling. She couldn't take all this in. 'And this treatment, is it working?' she asked carefully.

'We won't know for sure until a full two years from the first treatment has elapsed and they can do some conclusive tests.'

'And that will be in...?' she pursued gently.

'The beginning of November,' he said shortly, clearly wishing to change the subject. 'Now, let me take you through to get something to eat.' He had switched to urbane, smooth host again, the brief glimpse of the real man beneath the mask over. 'If the ravenous hordes have left anything for us.'

The ravenous hordes had—in fact there was enough food to feed a small army, Tamar thought weakly as she surveyed the wonderful spread laid out in the dining room, along with gallons of champagne to wash it down. When this man threw a party, he *really* threw a party.

Tamar noticed Emma and the earnest young man come through to the dining room some minutes later; he was pushing Jed's sister's chair and once he had her established in a protected spot he knelt down and talked to her for a moment or two, before standing and walking over to the buffet where he began to fill two plates.

'He still loves her.'

Tamar wasn't aware she had spoken out loud, but she must have done, because in the next instant Jed said, his voice peculiarly grim, 'Colin is the exception that proves the rule.'

'I'm sorry?' She looked up at him, her eyebrows raised.

'Colin Harding is first and foremost an academic,' Jed said quietly, 'and an intense individual in every way. But you're right; I do believe he loves Emma for herself. For one thing he is less interested in money and position than anyone else I know, and secondly, she is the only thing I've ever known him put before his precious books and research.'

'But why "the exception that proves the rule"?' Tamar persisted.

'Because love—romantic love between a man and a woman—is largely a figment of wishful thinking and people's imaginations,' Jed said coolly. 'It simply doesn't exist, except for the very rare exception, and even then, as in Colin's case, there are other factors involved.'

'You said he didn't care about Emma's money,' Tamar protested quickly, her face betraying her shock at his cynicism.

'I don't mean that.' He gestured irritably with his hand before saying, 'If Emma had married Ronald, and had a happy and successful marriage with a family and a secure lifestyle, Colin would have forgotten her long ago. As it was, with Emma's illness manifesting itself shortly after the wedding, and her all too obvious unhappiness with Ronald, she has continued to appeal to the illogical sentimental side of Colin. He sees himself as a knight in shining armour, ready to right all her wrongs and fight for a noble cause.'

'I've never heard anything so patronising in my life,' Tamar said forcefully, stiffening into a slender rod as she spoke, her eyes flashing.

'Then you haven't been around much,' he drawled scornfully, his own mouth thinning at her reaction and his eyes slits of silver in a face that had become devoid of expression.

'You're seriously telling me that just because Colin has continued to love her, even though she married someone else and probably broke his heart, you think he is fooling himself?' Tamar challenged in a soft hiss. 'I think that's insulting to both of them.'

Jed's eyes were glacial. 'Then don't think. You obviously aren't very good at it,' he bit out harshly.

'Because I disagree with you?' Tamar couldn't remember when she had last felt so mad. 'He loves her. Can't you just accept that? And people love other people the world over, for goodness' sake. You aren't really saying that millions of them are wrong and you alone are right, are you?'

'I'm saying they *think* they love each other,' Jed ground out softly, 'that's all. Emma thought she loved Ronald, but she didn't have a clue as to what made him tick. Her love was an illusion, a romantic fantasy wishful thinking had conjured up.'

'No, she fell in love with the wrong man, that's all,' Tamar shot back quickly. And to think she had begun to wonder if her first impressions of this man had been wrong! She had never met such an arrogant, heartless, condescending *swine* in all her life. 'But she obviously did love him, and hung on in there until she was forced to realise she had to let go. And for every Emma and Ronald, there are a hundred marriages that make a go of it.'

'Rubbish.' Jed's eyes narrowed in derisive contempt. 'If you are going to argue a point, at least get your facts straight. One out of three marriages end in divorce these days. That's a proven statistic.'

Well, she had walked into that one. 'I didn't mean a hundred literally,' Tamar admitted quietly, after taking a long, hard, calming breath and willing herself not to give way to the childish impulse to stick out her tongue. 'I was speaking metaphorically.'

'Well, don't.'

The impulse changed to a desire to kick him, hard.

'True love is one of the most dangerous illusions which has been perpetuated down the ages and right into the twentieth century,' Jed continued coldly. 'And the single cause of more heartache worldwide than all the wars and famines and natural disasters put together. In struggling to find something which doesn't exist, people load themselves and others with more hang-ups and trouble than the human spirit can take. How on earth can any rational human being expect to love one person, and one person only, for the rest of their lives?' he finished scathingly.

'You mean you couldn't,' Tamar interjected perceptively.

'What?'

She wasn't at all put out by his bark, which attracted veiled curiosity from those within earshot, and she certainly didn't intend to let his fierce scowl intimidate her either.

'You're a misogynist, pure and simple,' she said firmly, delighted she had got under his skin in some small measure.

'A...?'

'It means—'

'I know what it means,' he rasped tightly, 'and I can assure you I do not dislike women, Tamar, far from it. One day I shall marry, but my wife will be in no doubt as to why. I shall admire and respect her, and want her as the mother of my children, but as for love!' He glared at her contemptuously. 'It will be a legal contract to ensure my children are brought up in a happy and united home, and until they reach adulthood both my wife and myself will abstain from other partners. Once they are grown I should imagine we would go our separate ways. After twenty-odd years or so we would be sick of the sight of each other, although I hope we would remain friends for life.'

'I've never heard such a cold-blooded proposal in all my life,' Tamar gasped softly, truly shocked.

'No, it's merely honest. And my children, unlike many others, will not know the devastation of a warring home, and parents who make each other's lives hell on earth,' he said evenly. 'Now, finish your champagne and I'll fetch you another glass.'

'I don't want another glass.' Now was the moment to tell him about Gaby, that he had been wrong, criminally wrong about one woman at least, and that through his actions a life had ended before it had barely formed, with another one hanging in the balance for some hours. But she couldn't. She stared at him, her dark brown eyes enormous in the honey-cream of her face. She just couldn't. It might be letting Gaby down and betraying all her own ideals and convictions, and she might never have another chance like this again, but she couldn't bring herself to say the words.

Maybe if she couldn't see that wheelchair, and the frail, pathetically young-looking occupant, if the image of how Jed had looked at his sister, the love in his eyes, wasn't still stark on the screen of her mind, perhaps then she might have been able to accuse him. But he loved his sister, and his motives, cruel and ruthless though they had been, had been to protect Emma.

Not that that excused the sort of man he was, Tamar added quickly. It didn't—not at all. This last conversation was proof of the fact that he was the most cynical individual in the world. But... She sighed, finishing the last drop of sparkling effervescent wine and holding out her glass in silent capitulation. She couldn't do it and that was that. It had been a crazy idea from the start. All that remained now was to get through this evening as best she could, and then wipe Jed Cannon out of her mind and her life.

There was dancing to the small band in the grounds of the house later, the mellow, mild September night alive with the scents and smells of a dying summer. Hundreds of tiny fairy lights had been wound over trees and bushes, and they twinkled in the velvet darkness, creating their own ethereal enchantment for the evening as Jed led Tamar out of the over-warm confines of the house into the cool night.

He had remained at her side all evening, leaving only to replenish her plate and glass, and after that one soul-searing conversation had been charming. Tamar was aware of the many covert, and not so covert glances in their direction from interested parties—certainly most of the women present were agog to find out who she was and where she had come from—but with Jed standing at her side most people seemed loath to ask her any direct questions.

'Oh, it's beautiful out here.' Tamar stood still just outside the big French doors leading from the drawing room, quite entranced by the picture in front of her.

'It was the caterer's idea,' Jed drawled softly. 'As you have no doubt gathered, I haven't got a romantic bone in my body.' The dark eyebrows were mocking.

'I've gathered you don't like people to *think* you have,' she answered smartly. 'But methinks you protest too much.'

'Don't tell me—you took psychology at university.' He was teasing her. There was none of the constrained bitterness of their previous conversation, but her feelings had been sensitised by the emotion of the evening, and suddenly a remnant of the way she had felt during her university years swept over her, darkening her eyes to onyx as she recalled the pain and despair.

'English, actually.' She tried to match his lightness, but even she could hear the tremble in her voice.

She saw his eyes narrow on her tense face, and there was a moment of silence when she expected him to ask what was wrong, but instead he put out his hand and drew her gently into the side of him, his arm firm round her waist. 'Enough talking,' he said softly, his arm tightening to a band of steel when she would have pulled away. 'I have the feeling we're a couple who shouldn't talk at all.'

'We're not a couple,' she protested quickly, before she could stop herself.

'See what I mean?' He smiled, but the intent silver-grey eyes were piercing on her face. 'We're going to dance, Tamar, and I promise I won't say a word if you don't.'

'Jed, I don't want to…' But her protest was lost as he pulled her across the stone-slabbed patio directly out-side the drawing room doors and onto the bowling-green-smooth lawn, where several other couples were already dancing to a slow, dreamy number.

Her heart was beating rapidly as he pulled her closer to him, his hands about her waist so that her own were forced to rise and rest on his broad shoulders.

'This is nice.' He bent down and nuzzled her ear briefly, before raising his head again and looking straight into her flushed face. 'Don't you think?' he added mildly.

'Jed, I think you ought to know…'

'Yes?' They had begun to dance as she had spoken. 'What is it you think I should know?' he asked huskily, his dark face very tender.

'I'm not looking for any sort of a relationship at the moment.' She stumbled over the words, speaking too quickly but knowing if she didn't say it now, she never would. And it wasn't because she was waiting for an-other occasion when a rebuff would be more appropriate either, she admitted to herself. It was because…because being in his arms like this was too intoxicating, too dan-gerous. It made her want more, much more, and she had to deal with this thing that was beginning to take a firmer and firmer hold *now*.

'No?' He moved her even closer into his hard, masculine frame, so that her head rested against his chest and she could hear the steady beat of his heart through his shirt and jacket. The clean, wholesome smell of freshly laundered clothes mingled with the cool lemony scent of his skin and expensive aftershave. 'And you think I am?'

'I don't know,' she said with touching honesty, tilting back her head and looking straight into the mercurial silver gaze. 'But I think it's only fair to make it clear how I feel.' She knew her voice was breathless, but she couldn't help it; their bodies fitted together like the two halves of a jigsaw, as though they had been made for each other, and the little shivers running up and down her spine were interfering with her breathing.

'That's very brave.' She had lowered her head, but now raised it again abruptly, unsure if he was being sarcastic. But the dark face was very serious, his eyes showing something that could almost have been compassion. 'I could have said I'm not in the least interested, that you've taken too much on yourself,' he stated softly. 'Couldn't I?'

'Yes.' It was weak and wobbly, but the sensations turning her blood to liquid fire confirmed the necessity that this attraction was killed stone-dead.

'But we would both know that wasn't true,' he said almost thoughtfully. 'I do want you, Tamar. I want you very badly, as it happens, although I'm not quite sure why. You're very beautiful, but I meet a lot of beautiful women, and not one has affected me the way you have.

There's something about you...' He shook his head in mild self-derision. 'I can't explain it, even to myself.'

'Jed—'

'We need to talk about this privately.' He interrupted her trembling whisper by the simple expedient of drawing her away from the others into the soft shadows either side of the more brightly lit dancing area, moving swiftly into a small hidden circle of flowering bushes, which were perfuming the cool night air with the scent of mint and something exotic, before she could grasp what was happening.

'*No.*' She tried to pull away from him as he turned her to face him, but he merely drew her close again, kissing her forehead with warm lips.

'It's all right, don't panic. I'm not going to hurt you,' he said softly, one arm a band of steel about her waist and his other hand cupping her chin with exquisite gentleness. 'I'm not quite the ogre you have been led to believe.'

He was. And he wasn't. And she didn't know what she felt or believed any more, Tamar thought wretchedly. Except... Except she had to make sure she never saw him again.

'I want to go back to the others.' Strangely, in view of the circumstances, she didn't feel panic or distress, she realised shakily. He wasn't the sort of man who would force himself on a woman—she didn't know how she knew that, she just did. But she did feel fearful— although not at what Jed Cannon might do. No, her fear was all tied up in the self-knowledge of how she would respond to him if he started to make love to her. She wanted him. For the first time in her life she wanted a man's touch, his kisses...

'You don't want other people around any more than I do,' Jed challenged huskily. 'And when we talk things just get more complicated, right? So let's keep this simple...'

And now his mouth moved possessively over hers, but instead of the determined assault she was expecting his lips were sweet and tender, kissing her so expertly that she felt herself relax into his hard frame, a little sigh of pleasure escaping her mouth.

The sound of Jed's breathing was heavy and uneven, but it didn't register on her drugged senses for some minutes, and then, when she began to understand the control he was exerting, it caused her to kiss him back as she allowed him greater access to her inner mouth.

He groaned softly, the sound thrilling her as her body melted in liquid pleasure, and the night became midnight-blue behind her closed eyelids. He kissed her thoroughly, very thoroughly, taking his time and moving from a delicate and tantalising exploration of her mouth to a fierce, urgent plundering that had her shivering in response.

She was lost in the wonder of how she was feeling, and the rigid hardness in the big frame so close to hers told her Jed was aroused too. It ought to frighten her, Tamar told herself helplessly; since Mike Goodfellow's attack the knowledge of a man's arousal had become repugnant and alien, but this was different. *He* was different.

She knew her body was responding to him, and she knew he must be aware of it too, but somehow it didn't matter. Nothing mattered. And then the potential danger in that very thought broke through the euphoria like a

bucket of cold water, and she jerked backwards, taking
him completely by surprise.

'Don't.' She stared at him through the shadows, her
voice trembling and her eyes huge dark pools as she
instinctively placed the back of her hand across her
mouth. 'I don't want this.'

'I don't believe you.' It was matter-of-fact, not threatening, but then, as she took another step backwards, his
voice tightened as he said, 'For crying out loud, Tamar,
stop looking at me like that. I kissed you, that's all.'

It might have been nothing to him, but it had been
cataclysmic as far as she was concerned, Tamar thought
weakly, the knowledge making her suddenly terribly
vulnerable. He thought she was making a huge fuss over
nothing—it was there in the cool silver of his eyes, and
the way his mouth had thinned and straightened—but
she couldn't help the way she felt. She had allowed him
to kiss her, really kiss her, which was more than she had
done with any other man for years. But it wasn't just
that which was causing this feeling of panic. It was a
hundred other things, all tied up with the lazy authority
in that tall, male figure, the way he seemed to know
exactly what she wanted, the way he had *commanded*
her response. His power over her was terrifying.

She turned on the last thought, hearing his growl of,
'Tamar, what the hell...?' as she sped into the light,
winging her way across the lawn and into the house as
though the devil himself were after her.

After diving into the downstairs cloakroom, she bolted
the door after her and sat down with a little plop on the
small upholstered chair in front of the mirror, only then
realising she was shaking from head to foot.

He must think she was mad—stark, staring mad, she

told herself ruefully as she stared at her reflection in the mirror, noticing her full, swollen lips and flushed cheeks with a little sigh of despair. A kill like that would mean nothing to a man like him, but to her it had been one of the most intimate moments of her life. She sighed again, tears pricking at the back of her eyelids, before she straightened her back, and the stare changed to a glare.

'Right, Tamar McKinley,' she murmured softly, her eyes narrowing, 'that's enough. You are going to get back out there and act perfectly normal until you can order a taxi and leave with some dignity.' She nodded at the sombre reflection. 'And don't forget this is all your fault anyway. You should never have crossed swords with Jed Cannon. You just aren't in his league, girl.'

This fact was reinforced when, after some ten minutes or so, she had regained her equilibrium enough to leave her little sanctuary and venture out into the massive hall. The crowd had thinned a little, people had spread themselves out into the prettily lit night as well as the house, but there were still quite a few people left as Tamar tentatively emerged into the throng.

She had half expected Jed to be waiting for her—his face cold and angry and those riveting eyes expressing his disgust— but as she emerged he was nowhere to be seen. And then, as she moved slowly into the drawing room, and the crowd parted to reveal the garden beyond for a brief moment, she caught sight of him. And of the tall, willowy blonde hanging onto his arm and staring up into the dark, handsome features with adoring eyes.

She turned in one movement as the gaily dressed assembly blocked her view again, and was out of the front door before she even thought about it, walking down the long, winding drive with her head held high and praying that he wouldn't notice her leave.

She should have known, she should have *known*... There was an attendant on duty standing at the bottom of the drive near the gates, and the burly middle-aged man had a fatherly air as he tried to persuade her to wait until he called a taxi. 'It's a bit late for you to be walking about by yourself, miss,' he said worriedly. 'This is a better area than most, but you get the weirdos all places these days.'

'I'll be fine.' She managed a firm but appreciative smile. 'There's...there's someone picking me up just down the road.'

He didn't look as though he believed her, but he couldn't very well say so, and after one despairing glance in the direction of the party, now concealed by bushes and trees, he opened the gates and let her through into the quiet, sedate street beyond.

Tamar fairly flew along the pavement, her heart pounding, although it was less to do with the chance of the said weirdos appearing than a certain tall, silver-eyed millionaire in his gold Mercedes.

The road seemed endless, although she remembered from her previous visits before Jed had bought Greenacres that there was a very nice pub some three or four hundred yards away. Sure enough, as she rounded a slight bend in the road, there it was. It seemed in no time a taxi was drawing up at the pub door in answer to the telephone call the ruddy-faced publican had made for her, and she was on her way home...and out of Jed Cannon's life.

CHAPTER FIVE

'TAMAR? What the hell do you think you're playing at?'

She knew she should have let the phone ring, but she never had been able to do that, always fearing that the one time she did it would be a matter of life and death at the other end. But Jed sounded mad, blazingly angry...

'I searched the house and gardens for you I don't know how many times, and then Miles, my doorman, tells me that you left earlier. Are you *completely* stupid? Why the hell didn't you get my driver to take you home if you were in such a hurry to leave?'

'I...I ordered a taxi,' she said weakly.

'Where from?' he barked furiously. 'It wasn't my house, was it?'

She thought about lying, but he was so mad it didn't seem to make any difference, and so she admitted, 'The pub up the road.'

'"The pub up the road."' He echoed her voice in tones of utter disbelief. 'You mean to tell me you were so desperate to get away that you risked life and limb wandering about in the dark?'

'Hardly.' This was getting ridiculous, and she hadn't done anything wrong, Tamar thought rebelliously, apart from ducking out of his precious party, that was. And as far as she had been able to see he had quickly found other company to keep him happy. The thought of the beautiful blonde put strength back into her voice as she continued, 'The road is perfectly well lit, and it's now only—' she glanced at her little wooden wall clock '—half past ten.'

'Tamar, a young mother with two children in tow was molested only last week a few streets from here,' Jed said with bitingly cold control. 'How do you think I would have felt if something similar had happened to you?'

'I really don't know,' she answered in the same tone of voice he had used, 'but as I'm absolutely fine it isn't relevant one way or the other, is it?'

'What's the matter with you—?'

'Nothing is the matter with me,' she interrupted, with as much disdain as she could muster. 'I just don't happen to like men who invite a girl to a party and then think they have the right to paw her in return for a dinner and a drink or two.'

There was absolute silence on the other end of the phone, and then he said, his voice icy, 'Have you always been such a bitch, or have you been taking lessons?'

Tamar slammed down the receiver so hard it immediately jumped up again and took the whole telephone crashing to the floor, whereupon she burst into tears and sank down beside it.

She felt better after she had had a good cry, although she found she had given herself a thudding headache. After soaking in a long, hot bath for an hour, she blow-dried her hair into a riot of tumbling curls about her shoulders, donned her nightie, and went to bed with a mug of hot sweet milk and two aspirins. She had closed her mind to all thoughts of Jed Cannon when she was in the water, but found it less easy to stop him intruding once she was lying in a darkened room with sleep a million miles away.

She had made a complete and utter fool of herself tonight, she thought miserably, as she tossed and turned until the bed was a heap of tangled covers. She had planned to be so cool and elegant, so scathing when she told him what she thought of him, and instead she had reacted like a scalded cat when he had kissed her, and then further compounded the mistake by scuttling home like a frightened rabbit.

She thumped the pillow irritably, but no matter how she pummelled it into shape it seemed to have developed bricks inside.

He wouldn't contact her again, of course. He must think she was some sort of lunatic, and a bitchy one at that—his words had rankled far more than they should have done—but that was all to the good in the long run. Of course it was, she told herself firmly, her heart as heavy as lead. If she wasn't going to confront Jed about Gaby—and Tamar had to admit she wasn't at all sure if she could now she had seen Emma—then it was best she never set eyes on him again. And certainly after tonight he would have lost any interest he might have had in her. Which was good. Fine. Perfect. She thumped the pillow with enough force to knock out Mike Tyson.

The night dragged on, and eventually a gentle September dawn heralded a fine warm Sunday morning, the birds singing and chirping in the old grimy tree outside her bedroom window, as though they knew this was one of the last pleasant days before the onset of colder autumn weather.

It was a relief to rise and join the rest of the world, and after a shower and a hasty breakfast, of toast and grapefruit marmalade, Tamar donned a short-sleeved top and jogging trousers and went for a long run in the nearby park.

She saw several of the old regulars there, who usually made a weekend morning, and as always they joined together and ran in a group, exchanging banter and light-hearted gossip, before they all left the park and called in at Wilf's Café just round the corner for a second breakfast of wickedly high-calorie fried food.

By the time Tamar left the others she felt much more like her old self, and went home to enjoy a lazy afternoon with her feet up and the Sunday papers.

Olivia, Gaby's older sister by some ten years, phoned that evening, and, after they had exchanged news of a general nature, lowered her voice conspiratorially as she said, 'Has Gaby talked to you about this Peter Sinclair she's been seeing?'

'A bit,' Tamar answered cautiously. Olivia was a dear, but the difference in age meant she often behaved more like a mother than anything else with the two younger girls. Even her own growing family of two sons and two daughters didn't stop her taking an avid maternal interest in their lives. 'Why?'

'Well, he's gorgeous, absolutely gorgeous—not so much in looks, or anything, but as a person—you know? And he adores Gaby, dotes on her. It would be perfect if she felt the same way about him, don't you think?' Olivia asked probingly, knowing that Gaby had probably told Tamar far more about that side of things than her own sister.

Gaby had already confided that she thought Peter Sinclair might be more than just a friend, but that she was taking it very slowly after the devastation with

Ronald, which Tamar could understand. But she wasn't
going to tell Olivia that.

'Anyway, after all that's happened with that horrible
Ronald creep, Gaby deserves someone who will love her
and take care of her,' Olivia stated positively, when
Tamar wasn't forthcoming. 'I'd love to meet that swine
of a brother-in-law of his too. The air would turn blue,
I can tell you.'

'I doubt it,' Tamar responded drily. Olivia was just
about the most strait-laced thirty-four-year-old she had
ever come across. But she couldn't stop the sharp stab
of guilt that Olivia's innocent words had produced, and
long after the phone call had ended she sat in silent
contemplation, becoming more and more horrified that
she had been on the point, the night before, of making
love with the man who had caused such unhappiness to
her beloved cousin.

But she hadn't, not really, she argued with herself.
They had exchanged a few kisses, that was all.
Admittedly passionate kisses—oh, so wonderfully passionate—but just kisses. And in this day and age that
was nothing, absolutely nothing. There was no reason at
all for her to feel guilty. But Olivia's declaration continued to burn in her brain, each word a little arrow with
tips soaked in the poison of self-reproach and shame.

By the time she fell into bed at just after nine, exhausted by the lack of sleep the night before, Tamar had
promised herself fervently that she would never see Jed
Cannon again.

Not that he would suggest meeting her after the fiasco
of the previous night, she told herself miserably. But just
in case he did, she wouldn't.

And the funny little feeling the decision gave her, and

the vague depression her pledge induced, only confirmed she was right in the long run. He was the enemy and he was dangerous, and his power and authority was insidious. She had been lucky to get out when she did and have time to reflect and get herself together. It had nearly been too late.

Decision made, Tamar slept like a log, but when she awoke she knew her dreams—or certainly the last one, remnants of which had stayed with her long after her eyes were open—had been of a nature to make her blush, and that the main figure in the erotic fantasies had been tall and dark, with silver-grey eyes and a cruel ruthless mouth.

She was desperately glad it was a working day, and threw herself into the usual Monday morning mayhem with a single mindedness which brought overt approval from Fiona and Richard.

Tim was still full of gloom and doom at his girl-friend's exit from his life. He was tall, handsome and popular, and it was the first time in his twenty-five years that a female had finished with him; usually the boot was on the other foot. By lunchtime Tamar couldn't stand his mournful face a moment longer, and suggested they share a pub lunch together somewhere so that he could talk it through with an impartial third party. He agreed with alacrity, and so it was that the two of them left the office together, Tim taking her arm as they stepped into the street outside the building, and making her laugh as he called a cheeky farewell to Fiona and Richard.

'Tamar?'

The deep, husky voice caused her to freeze before she

turned slowly, Tim's arm still in hers and the smile dying from her face. It wasn't the Mercedes today, she noted numbly. Jed was sitting at the wheel of a beautiful red Ferrari, which was parked with magnificent unconcern for yellow lines a few feet away, and his face was imperturbable as he leant out of the open window.

'Hallo, Jed.' Amazingly her voice was cool and contained, betraying none of the sick agitation that had gripped her nerves at the sight of his cold handsome face.

'I'd like a word,' he said expressionlessly, for all the world as though she were alone.

The arrogance was colossal, and caught Tamar on the raw, causing her head to lift and her eyes to shoot sparks as she said, 'I can spare a moment or two. Or perhaps you would like to call me when I'm back in the office after two? I will have your file handy then.'

'Damn the file.' It had been a low growl, and then he seemed to catch himself, the intimidating mask sliding into place and his control back as he said smoothly, 'I'd like a word now, if you don't mind. And in private,' he added silkily, without acknowledging the other man by so much as the flicker of an eyelash.

'Unfortunately that's not possible.' She would rather walk on coals of fire than give in to such pretentious lordliness, Tamar thought furiously. Who *did* he think he was? 'I'm just on my way to lunch, with a friend.' She had left the barest pause before the last three words but it was enough to tighten the ruthless mouth into a straight line. 'Like I said, I'll be back in the office at two.'

Tamar was aware of Tim shifting uncomfortably at the side of her. The last thing she wanted was for him to encourage her to go with Jed, which she sensed he was about to do, and so after a sharp and very definite, 'Goodbye for now,' at the darkly angry occupant of the Ferrari, she turned quickly, almost lugging the unfortunate Tim along the pavement.

She half expected Jed to call after her, ordering her to stop, but he didn't, and when they had turned the corner she felt the air go out of her like a deflated balloon, and found she was leaning heavily on Tim's arm.

'What was all that about?' Tim made no pretence of tact. 'Are you seeing him or something?'

'No, I'm not seeing him, and there's no "something" either,' Tamar said forcefully. 'He's one of those men who thinks he only has to speak and the world stops to listen, that's all. Well, he's in for a bit of a shock where I'm concerned.'

Tim opened his mouth to speak, glanced again at her blazing eyes and ferocious scowl, and shut it again quickly. His mother was a redhead and he knew when to keep quiet. Nevertheless, the little encounter ruined the lunchtime interlude even as it succeeded in taking Tim's mind off his own troubles.

Tamar was on tenterhooks all afternoon, jumping visibly every time the telephone rang and tensing whenever the outer door opened. But he didn't ring and he didn't come to the office, and by six o'clock she had relaxed a little. Jed wasn't the type of man to continue to hit his head against a brick wall, she told herself reassuringly, and he must have got the message by now. And with all the other fish making sure they swam in his particular sea, he would have no trouble in selecting a suitable female to stroke that jumbo-sized ego.

She left the office at ten past six, noticing there was

a slight chill in the air that spoke of autumn although the day had been another warm one, and was just pulling her jacket—which she had been carrying over one arm— over her shoulders, when she became aware of the block of red on the perimeter of her vision. As though in answer to her glance, the Ferrari purred forward from its vantage point further down the street until it came to a halt just in front of her.

'Hi.' The window was down and Jed had one arm relaxed comfortably along its ledge as he spoke. He didn't smile.

Tamar didn't smile either as she nodded back at him, her eyes wary and her mouth straight.

'I've come to give you a lift home,' he drawled easily, 'so hop in.'

'I'd rather not, thank you,' she replied, without a change of expression.

'Don't be difficult, Tamar.' It was said with a light evenness, but there was steel underneath. 'Get in.'

She thought about defying him further, and then something about the set of his mouth, and a certain glint in the silvery eyes, warned her to go carefully. 'I don't want to argue with you—'

'Good, get in,' he interrupted frostily.

'But there's really no point,' she continued bravely. 'We said all that could be said last night, and—'

'Tamar, we said *nothing* last night,' he interrupted, for the second time in as many seconds, 'and there is no way I am leaving things as they are now. You are obviously of the impression that I am a cross between Don Juan and Jack the Ripper, and for some reason I can't fathom that bothers me.' The sarcasm was biting. 'Now, as I see it, you have two straightforward choices. You either get in this car voluntarily and allow me to see you home, whereupon we can discuss your…fantasies and bring them into the clear light of reason, or I can *make* you get in—gag you, tie you up. Whatever it takes to make you *listen* to me.'

His voice had risen during the discourse, something which he apparently was aware of as in the next instant he took a long, hard breath, pulling the air deep into his lungs, before he flexed powerful shoulders and added, his voice quiet now, 'The choice is yours.'

How had she got herself into this situation? Tamar stared at the sleek, powerful car, and the equally sleek, powerful occupant, as her mind raced. She knew he was quite capable of carrying out his threat to manhandle her into the vehicle. Of course she could cause a scene, shout, scream, but that would merely be acutely embarrassing for both of them, and if some stalwart citizen decided to call the police…

She got in the car.

'Why did you run from me like that last night?' It was soft and calm and not at all what she had expected.

She had been staring straight ahead, her hands clenched into tight fists at her sides and her back rigid as Jed eased the Ferrari into the tumultuous evening traffic, but at the sound of his quiet, even voice she relaxed a little, allowing her body to fall back in the seat as she said, 'I told you, I don't want to get involved with anyone,' and glanced his way.

'Does that anyone mean anyone, or just me?' he asked expressionlessly. 'You seemed on pretty good terms with that guy at lunchtime.'

'I work with Tim, that's all,' she defended herself quickly, before she had time to consider her words, and then immediately regretted she hadn't been cute enough to let him think she was interested elsewhere.

'I see.'

She had never travelled in a Ferrari before, and she couldn't really believe she was travelling in one now, especially with Jed Cannon. The car was everything it was purported to be, and a bit more besides, but it was more the dark, brooding presence of the driver that was turning her legs to jelly. His suit jacket was lying behind him and his dark ivory shirt was open at the collar, betraying a smidgen of dark curling body hair at the base of his throat. His shoulders were broad and muscled—he must work out, Tamar thought dazedly as she forced her gaze ahead again—and the long, lean frame seemed too large for the confines of the car. It was a powerful body, a very masculine body, and no woman could fail to feel the restrained force latent in the magnetic male sovereignty.

'Why don't you want to get involved with anyone, Tamar?'

She had been so concentrated on hiding what his nearness was doing to her shaky control that his soft voice made her start, and she moistened her lips, wiping her damp hands surreptitiously on the dark blue cotton of her skirt before she replied, 'I...I just don't, that's all.'

'That's no answer.' It was a command for more.

'I want to concentrate on my career,' she said shakily after a moment or two, 'and travel, see places. I want to please myself.'

'You could do all that with the right man,' he said evenly, 'and you know it. What was his name, Tamar? The man you loved and lost?'

'I haven't loved and lost anyone.'

It was so unmistakably the truth that Jed couldn't fail to recognise it as such, and he felt the frustration which had been steadily growing over the last few weeks since he had met this woman gnaw at his vitals.

'The man who hurt you, then?' he persisted softly, keeping his voice low and flat. 'Because someone did, didn't they?'

This was getting too close for comfort, and Tamar knew a moment of sheer panic. 'I don't have to want a man in my life, do I?' she snapped sharply. 'Thousands of women manage perfectly well without one, believe it or not.'

That was it. Someone *had* hurt her. He was surprised at how much the thought bothered him. What had happened? Had it been mental or physical abuse, or—and here he found he was grinding his teeth—something of a sexual nature? Whatever, it had cut deep; that was for sure.

'Perhaps.' His voice was purposely sceptical.

'You don't think a woman can exist happily without a man?' Tamar asked tightly.

'Oh, I think she can exist all right,' Jed drawled slowly. 'But happily...?'

'That's the most blinkered, chauvinistic rubbish I've ever heard,' Tamar said heatedly. 'I can't believe—' And then she caught sight of his face as he turned briefly and grinned at her. 'You're winding me up,' she said weakly.

'Me?' He shook his dark head slowly. 'Now would I?'

But it had defused what had been a painful moment for both of them, as Jed had meant it to.

It didn't take the powerful car long to reach Tamar's

apartment, although with the evening traffic at its height she could have walked it in about the same time. Jed cut the engine and settled more comfortably in his seat as he turned to face her, and she began the little speech she had been rehearsing for the last few minutes.

'I *did* enjoy the party on Saturday, Jed, and it was very kind of you to invite me,' she said primly. 'I just don't want to give you the wrong impression, that's all.'

'Forgetting the way you ran out on me like a frightened rabbit—' he noticed the way her mouth tightened at the analogy with secret amusement '—and your less than receptive reaction to my telephone call, what impression did you think you were giving that necessitated such…extreme clarification?' he asked with lazy mockery. 'I thought we were enjoying a relaxing evening among friends and getting to know each other better—'

'That's the thing,' she interrupted quickly. 'I don't want to get to know you—anyone—better.'

'You mean you don't want to have sex with me, Tamar.' It was a crude statement meant to shock, and it did, but Jed had just used up his meagre store of patience. 'But there was no question of that on Saturday night. It's obvious you will find this hard to believe, but I don't like promiscuity in either men or women, and I like my relationships to be built on friendship first and foremost.'

His *relationships*? How many did he have going? Tamar asked herself weakly as she stared at him, her face burning.

'I also like my women as eager as I am,' he continued quietly, 'with the choice, at all times, to say yay or nay. I have never forced a woman against her will, or even coerced one as far as I am aware, and I wouldn't start with you. There is much more to getting to know some-one than the physical act of intercourse,' he finished, his tone now expressing mild disappointment at her carnal mind.

'I know that,' she shot back quickly, stung at his in-sinuation that she'd only had one thing on her mind. 'Of course I know that.'

'But you thought I didn't?' he interjected smoothly, the calmness of his voice at odds with the rapier-sharp glitter in his eyes.

'No. Yes. Oh, for goodness' sake!' She glared at him angrily. How was it she had been made to feel like an immoral woman? she asked herself in amazement.

'All I wanted to do on Saturday night was this.' He dipped his head and took her mouth without waiting for an invitation, and this time the kiss was erotic and hard, his lips and tongue and gently savaging teeth creating an immediate whirlwind of sensation that had Tamar fluid beneath his onslaught. The kiss was endless, and at some time during it he moved her closer into him, leaning across her in the close confines of the car so that she was aware of every inch of his muscled frame, the rapid beat of his heart beneath the thin cloth of his shirt, the altogether male smell and feel of him.

And this time it was Jed who pulled away, moving back fully into his seat with a soft, regretful sigh before he said, his voice unforgivably steady and unconcerned, 'You see? Just a kiss, that's all.'

The second he moved away Tamar knew she should have resisted being in his arms, said something, done something, but the truth of the matter was that it simply hadn't occurred to her. Her whole being had been taken up with the amazing sensations in her traitorous body, which was still trembling from the feel of his hands and mouth. Her stomach felt warm and heavy, her breasts throbbing, her legs weak. Her eyes opened wider in alarm as the knowledge of just how she was feeling pressed the panic button. How could she want Jed Cannon to make love to her? How *could* she? Especially when it was patently obvious it didn't mean a thing to him.

'Now look—'

'I am looking,' he said with lusty appreciation. 'And even when I'm not looking I'm imagining *how* you look, and how you *would* look if I really made love to you. You're there all the time—in my shower, in the car, in my bed, the office...' He paused, his eyes wicked as he said, 'You're the first woman I've taken on my desk, Tamar, I can promise you that.'

'Jed—'

'At first I thought you were playing some sort of game,' he continued, almost thoughtfully, 'giving the wolf a taste, you know? But when you slammed the phone down on me it was genuine, wasn't it? And this lunchtime...I haven't had a woman treat me like that before.'

'No?' Self-preservation demanded sarcasm. 'How amazing.'

'Isn't it?' he agreed mockingly.

'How can you say all that, about your shower and...and everything—' she had been about to say 'and desk', but the image he had conjured up with his words was still so shockingly visible in her mind that she couldn't bring herself to name it '—and then say you want to get to know me slowly and not for just one thing?' she demanded hotly.

'I'm being truthful, that's all,' he stated with suspect righteousness. 'I *do* want to get to know you as a person, that's very important in any relationship, but I also want you physically—with a desire that is driving me mad. There, cards on the table.' He smiled, with a boyish sweetness that swept away all the hard cynicism for a brief moment and made him look as he must have done at eighteen.

It hit her hard, like a well-aimed punch in the solar plexus, and in the same instant she faced the fact that if things had been different—if there had been no Gaby, no miscarriage, and for her personally no Mike Goodfellow—she would have taken the plunge and risked venturing into Jed Cannon's world. But things weren't different, and, Gaby or no Gaby, she didn't have the expertise, the knowledge, or the self-confidence and belief in herself to handle a man like him.

He would chew her up and spit her out and then go on to the next woman with a warm farewell and a wish that they would still be friends. An impossible affair.

'I'm sorry, Jed.' She had been unaware of the intense scrutiny behind the steady silver eyes as he had watched her face whilst keeping perfectly still. 'But I meant what I said.'

'So did I.' But the smile had gone as he continued, 'And I want you, Tamar.'

He spoke as if the mere wanting made the outcome inevitable, and something he had said on his decision to purchase Greenacres—and which she now repeated in a slightly shaky voice—flashed into her mind. 'And you have always prided yourself on being a man who knows what he wants when he sees it, and then acquires it?' she said, with a hostile lift of her chin.

His eyes narrowed, his brow wrinkling for a brief moment before clearing as he nodded slowly. 'I was referring to possessions rather than people when I said that,' he qualified coolly, 'but the cap fits and I'm happy to wear it.'

'Are you indeed?' She glared at him, her voice taut as she said, 'Well, it might surprise you to know that I don't like being put in the same category as a new suit or pair of shoes, or even a house as magnificent as Greenacres. I'm a flesh and blood person, in case you hadn't noticed, and I think your philosophy on life and love stinks.'

'That's not very liberal of you.'

His voice was dry and mocking, but if she had been watching closely—which she wasn't, her rage making her blind to everything but the force of her own feelings—she would have seen his face had straightened at her words, and a pulse beating in his throat that betrayed he was not as relaxed and imperturbable as he would have liked her to believe.

'Like you, I'm being truthful, that's all,' she flashed back tightly, repeating his earlier words with disdainful contempt.

'So much anger and hostility.' Suddenly he was deadly serious, folding his arms across the muscled expanse of his chest as he surveyed her from piercing eyes. 'Why?'

'Just because I don't want to sleep with you does not make me angry or hostile,' she returned sharply, and then, realising she had to take control of both the situation and herself, she drew in a deep, shuddering breath and said, 'Look, this is getting us nowhere. Thank you for the lift, but I really don't think there is any point in us meeting again. Of course, if you need Taylor and Taylor in a professional capacity, please do not hesitate to phone—'

'Eight o'clock.'

'What?' He had cut her off in mid-flow, and now she stared at him as he eyed her impassively.

'Eight o'clock. I've got two tickets for the theatre and I'll pick you up at eight. Okay?' he drawled lazily.

'No, it is not okay.' She really couldn't believe they were having this conversation after all that had gone before. The whole thing was becoming surreal. 'I've told you—'

'I'll pick you up, take you to the theatre and then straight home afterwards without so much as holding your hand. How about that?' The beautiful eyes smiled at her and she wanted to melt.

'Jed, I don't want to be difficult, but—'

'Then don't be,' he encouraged promptly.

'And please don't keep interrupting me,' she snapped, her irritation at his despotic attitude sweeping away the momentary weakness his smile had induced. 'I really don't want to go out with you.'

'I know.' There was an inflexion in his voice that caused her eyes to connect sharply with his, but she could read nothing in the bland, cool features and decided she must have imagined the throb of what she had thought was bitterness. 'But you'll enjoy it when you do.'

She stared at him for a full minute, the sounds from the warm September night outside the car barely penetrating the luxurious interior, before she said at last, her voice flat, 'You aren't going to take no for an answer, are you?'

'The word doesn't feature in my vocabulary,' he agreed softly.

'And you meant what you said about it being platonic?' she pressed as she looked into the hard, handsome face.

'If that's the way you want it.'

'It is,' she said quickly, nodding to emphasise the point.

'So be it.' He stretched, and a hundred warning bells began to ring as the long, lean frame touched every nerve in her body whilst remaining a good twelve inches away. 'But I'm a great believer in a lady being able to change her mind,' he said silkily.

'This one won't.' She eyed him militantly.

'I wouldn't bet on that, Tamar.' He ignored her scornful 'huh' as he continued, 'Perhaps not tonight, perhaps not even the next time I take you out, but soon, very soon, you'll want me just as much as I want you...'

CHAPTER SIX

IF TAMAR had had to say the next morning, hand on heart, whether she had enjoyed the evening at the theatre, the answer would have been a reluctant yes, and following that date there were three more.

The first was Sunday lunch, followed by an afternoon drive, and then a quiet, cosy evening in a wonderfully old-fashioned pub Jed knew, with horse brasses on the walls and low, exposed beams which caused every male over six foot to duck his head.

The second, a music festival on the outskirts of London, had some of the most famous names in the entertainment world present, and left Tamar in no doubt that Jed knew everyone and anyone.

But it was the third, a quiet romantic dinner for two at Greenacres, when they were waited on by Jed's newly acquired housekeeper and then left strictly alone, which convinced Tamar her exit from Jed Cannon's life had to be like the surgeon's knife—swift and unflinching, with the emphasis on swift.

Not that he hadn't behaved like the perfect gentleman, she reminded herself unhappily, the following morning after the dinner. He had—on all three dates. Not a word, not a gesture out of place, and definitely no body contact or anything that could be faintly misconstrued. Perversely it had irritated her far more than she could have expressed. She wanted... Oh, she didn't know what she wanted, she admitted miserably, only what she had to do. And that was make sure this brief interlude ended once and for all.

She wrote the letter before she had time to hesitate— a strong no-nonsense letter which would toll the death knell on any relationship and penetrate even Jed Cannon's special brand of arrogance—and posted it on her way to work.

'Nice time yesterday evening?' Fiona and Richard had been watching events with avid curiosity and not a little amazement, their all too obvious puzzlement at Tamar's refusal to get excited at Jed's interest forcing her to tell them the whole story after the second date. Fiona had made no bones about the fact that she thought Tamar ought to let bygones be bygones, her magnanimity prompted less by Jed's extenuating circumstances and more by the size of his bank balance, Tamar suspected.

This morning Fiona had pulled her into the little kitchen at the back of the building as soon as Tamar had stepped through the door, and now her friends's eyes were bright with interest as she added, 'Was his sister there?'

'No one was there, except the housekeeper,' Tamar said flatly.

'I thought so.' Fiona nodded wisely, pursing her lips and narrowing her eyes. 'He means business, Tamar. I really think you've hooked him.'

'I don't *want* him,' Tamar insisted forcefully.

'You do, you just don't know it yet.' Fiona smiled, with such patronising condescension that Tamar could have hit her— friend or no friend. 'It needed someone like Jed Cannon to bring you out of that glass tower you've inhabited for the last few years.'

'*I haven't!*' Tamar was stung into raising her voice. 'How can you say that, Fi?'

'Because it's true,' Fiona said quietly, her eyes compassionate as she looked at the beautiful angry face in front of her. She couldn't remember the number of times she had wished Mike Goodfellow to a place where it was very hot and very final. When he had ripped his way into Tamar's body he had taken more than just her virginity, and she and Richard had been full of admiration for the way the slender, gentle girl in front of her had fought back from such a crippling experience. But she still wasn't over it yet, Fiona thought perceptively, although Tamar would refute that.

'Well, whatever you say, I've finished it this morning.' Tamar stared at her for one moment more, before turning away with a shrug of her shoulders. 'Rightly or wrongly, I've written him a letter which he'll receive tomorrow morning, so that's that.'

'He won't accept it,' Fiona stated positively.

'He'll have to.'

The first bouquet arrived at the office on Tuesday lunchtime—the morning Jed would have received the letter. The twenty-four red roses were just beginning to open their crimson petals, and reduced the worldly-wise Fiona to a gushy mess as she eyed Tamar holding the flowers. The card read simply, 'That word still isn't in my vocabulary.'

'Oh, this is *so* romantic.' Fiona was captivated. 'Richard never did anything like that for me.'

'I never had to,' Richard said stolidly. 'I couldn't get you out of my life or my bed from the first week we met.'

The next morning brought a huge posy of fragrant freesias edged with baby's breath, which perfumed the office all day, and the message, 'Thinking of you.'

Thursday it was three dozen stems of Regal lilies, the gently scented, white funnel-shaped flowers with their brilliant yellow centres taking up all one corner of the office and staring accusingly at Tamar all day as she tried to work. The card read, 'Royal flowers for a princess,' and had Fiona sighing blissfully into her coffee.

Tamar hardly dared to turn up for work on Friday. Her flat resembled a flower shop, and the smell was overpowering, but it was the way Jed's persistence was affecting her that really troubled her. She wanted to feel annoyed or irritated, certainly exasperated at his tenacious pursuit, but instead there was a bubble of something deep inside that caused the sky to look bluer and the air to smell fresher, even as she acknowledged an underlying thread of unease. Because all this could only have one conclusion. And it wasn't just the fact she would never be able to look Gaby in the eye again if she allowed Jed Cannon to invade her life.

It was *him*. Tamar stopped abruptly on the pavement just outside the office, ignoring the October drizzle as she examined her thoughts. He had made it crystal-clear how he viewed any association with her, and love and commitment would never enter into it. Oh, she didn't doubt he would remain faithful for as long as the affair continued, but one day it would end. He had already said so. Ninety-nine women out of a hundred might be able to cope with such cold-blooded honesty, but she wasn't one of them.

Her shoulders slumped and her head bowed, and then she caught sight of her reflection in the window and straightened immediately, a thread of angry self-disgust blowing away the momentary weakness. She had never cried for the moon in the past, or worn her heart on her sleeve, and she didn't intend to start now. She forced a smile to her face and refused to let her thoughts go any further, opening the door with a cheerful, 'Good morning, everyone.'

It was deep red carnations later that morning, just before the coffee break, and the rich blooms were snuggled in a cloud of forget-me-nots. 'I have it on good authority that in the language of flowers red carnations stand for "alas for my poor heart",' Jed had written, 'and the forget-me-nots are self-explanatory.'

Alas for my poor heart? Tamar stared at the card as a flood of anger rose, sweeping away the unease in a fiery river. This was all a game to him, an interesting and diverting game, but a game nevertheless. Forget the flowers, the cards, the sweet talk—he wanted to bed her and that was his only intent. She said as much to Fiona, who was oohing and ahhing as normal.

'But of course, darling, men are all the same,' Fiona agreed brightly. 'You really couldn't expect anything else. The trick is keeping him interested *afterwards*, and you are bright enough, and beautiful enough, to do that.'

'He doesn't want a permanent relationship,' Tamar insisted firmly. 'He's already said as much.'

'Well, you might not after a time,' Fiona said reasonably. 'Can't you just enjoy yourself for a change, and hang the future?'

No, she couldn't do that. Tamar stared at the other woman, her eyes wide with the horror of sudden self-awareness. Because she loved him. *Some time over the last two months she had fallen in love with Jed Cannon.*

'What's the matter?' Fiona took a step towards her, her voice urgent as she looked into Tamar's stricken eyes. 'Do you feel ill? Tamar, what is it?'

On the perimeter of her consciousness Tamar was aware of the outer door opening and closing, and of a shadowy figure entering the office, but it wasn't until Richard's voice said, 'Mr Cannon, this is a pleasant surprise,' that her startled gaze swung from Fiona's face to that of the tall dark man, who was watching her so intently.

'Hallo, Tamar.' He spoke softly, and the deep, husky voice trickled over her skin as though he was already touching her.

Tamar was powerless to make any reply, the shock of her discovery and the physical presence of the figure who had occupied most of her waking moments and all of her dreams for the last few weeks rendering her speechless, and it was Fiona who moved forward, a hundred-watt smile on her face as she said, 'Mr Cannon? How do you do? I don't think we've been formally introduced. I'm Fiona Taylor, and this is my husband, Richard.'

'Tamar's friends, yes. She has often spoken of you.'

He was smiling down at Fiona, all charm and white teeth, but Tamar still couldn't move or take her eyes off his face. The black straight brows, the riveting eyes, the all-encompassing magnetic power that radiated around him like a dark aura. Why was he here? Right now? Had he somehow sensed what she was feeling? Known she was at her weakest and moved in for the kill?

The ridiculousness of the thought provided the dose of adrenalin she needed to pull herself together. He was egotistical enough as it was; he would just love it if he sensed she was bestowing super-human qualities to him.

'Hallo, Jed.' She managed a somewhat shaky smile, but was pleased at the coolness of her voice. 'No problem with Greenacres, I hope?'

'None that I'm aware of,' he said smoothly. 'I've called in about my apartment, actually. I'd like Taylor and Taylor to put it on the market for me.'

'Oh, yes?' Tamar had seen the glance that had flashed between Fiona and Richard, and she knew exactly what they were thinking, especially as Fiona compounded the gesture by peering covetously out of the window at the majestic Mercedes parked regally outside, the chauffeur sitting impassively behind the wheel. Multimillionaires didn't condescend to visit like this. The most they could have hoped for was an imperial summons, followed by five minutes of his time. He had come to see Tamar. They all knew it.

Jed nodded, the silver eyes fastening on Tamar's flushed face. 'I don't really need two properties so close together, and Greenacres is becoming more like home every day. So...I've a spare hour or so this morning if you're available?'

He had phrased it as a question, but they both knew it was more in the nature of a command, and it was clear Fiona knew which side the firm's bread was buttered as she quickly offered, 'That's fine, absolutely fine. I can take your appointment with Mrs Carstairs, Tamar.'

Fait accompli. As Jed had meant it to be—as he had known it would be. Money talked, and nowhere so distinctly as in this man's orbit, but if he thought he could buy her he was mistaken. She would go with him and value his darn flat, but that was all she would do.

'Fine.' Tamar echoed Fiona's words with a brittle smile. 'I'll drop everything and come with you right now, then, shall I?'

'If you don't mind,' he said evenly, but Tamar had seen her veiled sarcasm register in the piercing eyes and knew he hadn't liked it.

Tim had kept quiet all through the little exchange, but now he surprised everyone—including himself, if the faintly desperate look in his sky-blue eyes was anything to go by—when he said, looking straight at Tamar, 'I'm free this morning. Would you like me to come with you and take down the particulars?'

'I don't think one apartment necessitates taking up the valuable time of two of your employees?' Jed interposed swiftly as he turned to glance at Fiona and Richard.

'No, of course not,' Fiona agreed quickly, casting a warning glance from under her eyelashes at Tim, who was clearly in white knight mode.

Whether he didn't see Fiona or chose to ignore her was uncertain, but Tim again looked straight at Tamar as he said, 'Tamar? I can catch up on any work tonight if you'd like me to come with you.'

'No, it's all right, Tim. But thank you,' Tamar said softly, touched by the young man's genuine concern for her but wanting an end to what had become an acutely embarrassing moment. She could see Jed's face was as black as thunder, and so could Fiona and Richard, and she knew Tim was going to be in hot water once she'd left. 'I appreciate the offer,' she added quietly, her eyes warm as she smiled at him before turning and reaching for her jacket and handbag.

Once they were seated in the back of the Mercedes she willed the hot colour in her cheeks to subside and sat quietly, saying nothing. The silence went on and on, stretching and lengthening until the air was crackling with electricity, but Tamar was determined she wasn't going to speak first.

It was a good five minutes before Jed said, his voice taut, 'I thought there was nothing between you and the boy back there?'

He made it sound as though Tim was still in short pants, and Tamar warned herself not to bite back, speaking coolly and evenly as she answered briefly, 'There isn't.'

'You could have fooled me.'

'Really?' she said tartly. 'That must be a first.'

'Tamar.'

'And stop trying to bully me,' she snapped hotly, the resolve of a few seconds before burnt up in the tumult of emotion that was turning her inside out. Until he had walked into the office she hadn't realised how much she had *ached* to see him, but now he was here, in the flesh, and she was finding it physically painful, the pressure in her heart unbearable.

'*Bully* you?' he echoed tightly.

'Yes, bully me.' She made the mistake of turning to glare at him, and then wished she hadn't. In the close confines of the car he looked good enough to eat, his big black overcoat and wind-ruffled hair emphasising the dark sexiness which lay at the root of his attractiveness. 'Barging in there like that and ordering me to come with you, and the flowers all week and everything.'

'You see the flowers as a way of my bullying you?' he snarled incredulously.

'Intimidating me, then,' she qualified tautly.

'I don't believe this.' He had been sitting forward in

the seat but now he lay back, taking a long, deep, hard breath before he said slowly, 'Tamar, the flowers weren't meant to bully you or intimidate you or anything else of that nature. I just don't understand…' He paused, raking his hair back from his brow before he continued in a low growl, 'I don't understand how to *reach* you, that's all.'

Oh, no, don't do this. Don't do lost and uncertain on me, she prayed silently, the twist her heart had given at his admission stopping her breath.

'And coming here today like this…' He paused again, and then turned to look at her, his voice full of self-derision as he continued, 'I was sitting in my office and I couldn't let another hour go by without seeing your face. Big joke, eh? You can go back there and give them all a good laugh now, can't you?'

'I wouldn't do that,' she said numbly.

'No, I know you wouldn't,' he agreed softly. 'Because you aren't like that, are you? I mean you *really* aren't like that. There are any number of women I know who would be milking this for all it's worth, getting the most out of me they could, but you haven't asked me for a damn thing.'

'Of course I haven't.' She was shocked to the core and it showed.

He leant forward abruptly, pulling down the blind over the glass which separated them from his driver and then turning back to her, his eyes softer than she had ever imagined they could be as he said, 'How have you reached the age of twenty-four in this big, bad world and stayed like you are?'

It was a stupid question—and she knew she shouldn't

ask it—but she found herself saying, her voice weak and trembling, 'How am I?'

'Perfect,' he said huskily. 'Absolutely perfect.'

He pulled her into his arms in one swift movement, crushing her against him as he groaned her name against her lips which opened obediently beneath his searching mouth. His tongue was erotic in the warm, secret places of her mouth, and she could feel the thrusting arousal of his body against her softness as he moulded her even closer, his fingers tangling in her hair, the silky red-gold curls tumbling about her shoulders as they escaped their combs.

This was the middle of a Friday morning in busy London traffic.

The same thought must have occurred to Jed, because in the next instant he had reluctantly drawn back, his breathing heavy and laboured as he looked down into her flushed face. 'See? See what little control I have where you are concerned,' he said softly. 'You are like a drug. I can't get enough of you.'

'Jed—'

'And all this "don't touch, hands off" is driving me crazy. I want you, Tamar. I can't believe how much I want you. And you want me. You might not like it, but you want me. Is this the end of the hide and seek? Are you ready to admit that there's a fire that burns between us every time I touch you?'

She didn't try to answer him, persuading the wild disarray of her hair back into the small tortoiseshell combs Jed's fingers had dislodged, her hands trembling.

'Come and stay the weekend at Greenacres,' he said huskily.

'What?' Luckily the last comb was firmly in place as her head swung sharply to face him.

'Emma wants to see you again.' And then, as she slanted her eyes in disbelief, he raised a sardonic black eyebrow. 'You don't believe me?' he asked amusedly.

'No, I don't,' she admitted drily, willing the pounding of her heart to slow down and hoping he couldn't see the turmoil she was still in. How could he make her feel like that with just a kiss? He'd talked about a fire burning between them, and the wild, hot pain surging through her body felt akin to being burnt.

'Don't beat about the bush, Tamar, feel free to be honest,' he said sarcastically. And then, when she continued to eye him without speaking, 'It *is* the truth, as it happens. She really liked you, you know, and she's asked about you more than once. The next few weeks are going to be difficult ones for her as we get nearer to knowing whether the treatment has been successful or not, and it would be good for her to have another woman to share some of her fears with. Ronald cut her off from most of her friends during the course of their marriage, and she hasn't got anyone she can really talk to.'

'She's got you,' Tamar said carefully, 'and Colin Harding.'

'But that's not like another female, is it?' Jed argued softly. 'She could probably say things to you she wouldn't dream of telling me.'

'Don't do this, Jed.' She stared at him, her eyes pleading with him. 'Don't try and make me feel guilty. We both know why you want me to stay the weekend.'

'Shame on you, child.' He grinned at her, bending swiftly to kiss the tip of her nose. 'Carnal thoughts again?' But the silver eyes were still hot with desire, and his body was betraying the passion that had him in its grip. 'Look, Tamar, you'll have your own room, with a lock and key if you like, how about that? Just one weekend—surely that's not too much to sacrifice for someone who needs you desperately, is it?'

She wasn't sure if he was referring to Emma or himself, and she shook her head slowly as she said, 'I would have thought blackmail was beneath you.'

'Me?' The grin deepened. 'Oh, no, not where you are concerned. Anything it takes, Tamar, anything it takes.'

They said nothing more until the Mercedes pulled up outside the beautiful old building in Kensington where Jed's apartment was situated, the regal and somewhat imperious frontage disguising—at first glance—how huge the structure was. A minor concession to the twentieth century had been made in the lobby, with the installation of lifts to the eight apartments the building housed, but as the doorman escorted them to the lift, making small talk with Jed, Tamar gained an overall impression of tasteful elegance and peace and quiet more reminiscent of a bygone age.

Jed's apartment was the penthouse, and huge. As soon as Tamar walked into the Gothic-style hallway, with its stone fireplace, she knew this was not going to be the flamboyant bachelor pad she had prepared herself for but a real home, and that another preconceived idea about the man beside her was going to be blown away.

She was right. From the old Victorian mirror above the Haddonstone fireplace in the magnificent blue and gold drawing room, to the nineteenth-century dining chairs covered in Honan silk in the cream and claret dining room, the apartment breathed beauty and warmth.

Besides the drawing room and dining room, there was

another reception room, a large book-lined study, and a massive combined breakfast room and beautifully fitted kitchen, along with four double bedrooms and two bathrooms.

'It's gorgeous.' They were standing in what was obviously the master bedroom—a very male room in grey and green, with the most enormous four-poster bed covered in antique French raw-linen bed sheets, complete with personal monograms, and a polished wood floor—and now, more to take her mind off the bed than anything else, Tamar said, 'You haven't used any of this furniture for Greenacres. Are you intending to sell it?' in a small, slightly awed voice.

'No.' He was leaning against the far wall, his hands thrust into the pockets of his trousers and his narrowed eyes tight on her face. 'I'm toying with the idea of looking for a country retreat, or even a place down in Cornwall, close to the sea, so until I make up my mind one way or the other this lot will go into storage.'

'Right.' She nodded carefully, still pretending to look at the pictures on the walls, the furniture, anything but the dark, brooding figure across the room.

'I have a place in Malaga I can escape to now and again,' he continued quietly, his husky voice making her nerve-endings jump, 'but a sanctuary in England would be nice too.'

'You feel you need a sanctuary?' she asked in surprise, glancing his way.

'Doesn't everyone?' he returned softly.

'Yes, but you seem... Well, you're not...' Her voice trailed away as the steel-grey eyes held hers.

'Yes?' he probed intently. 'How do I seem, Tamar? How do you see me? As a robot, perhaps? Some sort of super-human machine that doesn't need the normal things other men need?'

'I didn't say that,' she defended herself quickly.

'You don't have to.' He levered himself off the wall, walking over to her with an easy animal grace that was very masculine and very threatening. 'I now know enough about you to appreciate there is a very soft heart beating under that amazingly beautiful exterior,' he said, with a soft grimness that had her eyes transfixed on his face. 'But where I am concerned you are on the defensive one hundred per cent of the time, and have been from the first moment we met. You don't like me, Tamar. Why?'

'I've never said that—'

'Oh, you're attracted to me...physically,' he continued darkly, 'but that's all.'

If he did but know. If he did but *know*. Tamar stared at him, her mouth dry. But he mustn't guess—not ever—the way she felt about him.

'Why haven't you ever given me a chance, Tamar?' he asked quietly. 'What have you heard about me that has filled you with such suspicion?'

Now was the moment to tell him the truth, to explain about Gaby and Ronald and how she had felt, Tamar told herself wretchedly. She could tell him quietly, rationally, explain her feelings then, and how, after meeting Emma and understanding his motives, she felt now. But she couldn't. She just couldn't.

She continued to stare at him, her mind racing. As things were now, he thought she didn't like him, and that gave her some sort of protection. If she told him the truth that shield would be gone, and even if he didn't guess her true feelings for him he would know she had mellowed. And that would be fine, just fine, if there was the slightest hope he could ever want her for more than just a passing bed partner. But he wouldn't. He had nailed his colours to the mast within days of them meeting, and if she allowed herself to get involved with him she would have no one to blame but herself when he left. And he would leave. How could she, Tamar McKinley, ever hope to keep a man like Jed Cannon interested?

'I don't know. You…you've got something of a reputation, I suppose,' she managed at last, her voice shaking.

'I can buy that.' He nodded soberly, moving closer and staring down at her musingly, his face veiled now and strangely expressionless. 'But you aren't prepared to look beyond the reputation, to give me a chance?'

'It…it wouldn't work. You must know that,' she prevaricated weakly. 'We're so different—our outlook on life and everything.'

'I don't agree.' And then he shocked a startled gasp out of her when he said, coolly and with no emotion, 'Are you a virgin, Tamar? Is that why you're so frightened of this passion between us?'

'I… How can you…?'

'Are you?' he persisted softly, quite unmoved by her red face and helpless splutterings.

She took a deep breath, the pain biting deep as she said, 'No, I'm not a virgin, Jed.' And somehow, in spite of all the years in between and how far she thought she had come, the stark anguish and despair and humiliation overwhelmed her for a brief moment.

'What is it?' He had seen the look on her face and it had appalled him, but when she didn't speak the seething cauldron of baffled frustration and bitterness boiled over, and he pulled her to him so abruptly her head snapped back on her shoulders. 'For crying out loud, *talk* to me,' he snarled furiously. 'Say something—anything. Lie if you want to, but give me a reason for how you are.'

'Let go of me!' Suddenly it was Mike Goodfellow in front of her, and she began to fight and kick in the way she had all those years ago. But this time there was no hard blow across her face to stun her for precious lost moments, or brutal hands tearing the clothes off her back.

Instead he simply held her to him, taking the battering of her hands and feet without moving, his body still, with a whipcord hardness which spoke of restrained power and strength.

How long she continued to twist and struggle she didn't know, but when eventually she became quiet she would have fallen at his feet but for his hands holding her up. And it was long minutes later, when the shuddering sobs racking her body had died away to hiccuping gasps, that he said, his voice thick and husky, 'How long have you been holding on to all that?'

What had she done? Her eyes were shut tightly, her face burning. How could she have behaved like that? Never, even in the worst moments of desperation and misery following the attack, had she lost control. She hadn't dared to. To be in control—of herself and every situation about her—had become of prime importance in a world that had been turned upside down. And now she hadn't only lost control but had physically attacked him... 'I'm sorry,' she whispered dully.

'Forget it.' He was still holding her, his hands moving slowly up and down her arms in an attempt to comfort.

'No, I mean it. I...I never behave like that,' she murmured helplessly. 'It...it wasn't you. You know that, don't you?'

'It felt like me.' It was rueful but not unkind. In fact his voice had a tender note that made her want to cry again. 'Do you want to talk about it?' he asked softly, as her lower lip trembled.

'No.' Yes, yes, I want to talk about it, to make some sense of the feelings that still rip me apart if I let myself remember, but I *can't*. 'I'm all right now.' She raised her head as she spoke and then stilled at the look in his eyes, time standing still as they gazed at each other in the quiet, sun-dappled room, the weak October sun outside the window casting golden sunbeams across the mellow wood floor.

Tamar's mouth was dry, she was unable to utter a word, and when the kiss came it was delicate, sensuous, stroking a response that came shivering up from the depths of her and was impossible to deny. The warm moistness of his tongue began to trace the outline of her soft, full lips in an evocative caress that was more erotic than any blatant passion, probing gently until they parted and allowed him entry to her mouth.

And then she began to kiss him back. She couldn't help it, his gentle sensuality igniting a reaction that was pure pleasure. He didn't hurry, in spite of her reaction, taking his time as he slowly explored the warm cavities of her mouth until she was trembling with desire, her hands unresisting against the broad expanse of his chest and her head tilted back as she whimpered softly against his lips.

'So beautiful, so exquisite...' His voice was like raw silk on her sensitised emotions, and she moaned her need of him, moving into the male hardness of his muscled body without being aware of what she was inciting.

She wasn't conscious of Jed moving her to the bed— although he must have done—but, caught up in the wonder of his skilful lovemaking and her own uninhibited response, she wouldn't have been able to resist anyway.

He removed her jacket and his own coat with a smooth adeptness that should have set the alarm bells ringing, but Tamar was in a different world—a world of fierce, driving need and throbbing sensation that had nothing to do with real life.

His hands increased the heady, surging rhythm his mouth had begun, the blood singing through her veins and a low sweet ache at the pit of her stomach building moment by moment until she moaned helplessly. Jed's throaty breathing was an aphrodisiac in itself, and one which excited her more than she could have imagined, the need he was betraying—his flagrant desire— inflaming her passion into a whirling kaleidoscope of colour behind her closed eyelids.

His hands were knowing as they slid over her body, and thrillingly capable of firing all the right buttons, her breasts becoming heavy and swollen and their hard, pointed tips thrusting against the soft wool of her dress. She was gasping his name in between the fire of their kisses, utterly surrendered to his will, so when his touch became restraining rather than sensuous, and then finally stopped, until he was just holding her against him, she opened drugged eyes to stare at him bewilderedly.

'What's the matter?' she whispered shakily as she stared into the darkly brooding face above her, becoming aware in the same moment of just what she had allowed and how intimately close they still were, their bodies touching length against length and every bone and muscle in that hard frame known to her.

'Another minute and I wouldn't have been able to stop,' he growled huskily. 'You understand me, Tamar? And you're not ready for this yet, are you? When I have you it will be because you want *me*, Jed Cannon, and not just because of how I can make you feel in bed either. And afterwards there will be no doubt that you knew exactly what you were doing.'

Tamar stared at him, unable to believe what she was hearing, her eyes blank. What had this been? she asked herself in horror. An exercise to prove who was in control here? A way of showing her that he could take her or leave her, as he chose? And she had played right into his experienced hands. All her fine words, all her righteous protestations of moralistic restraint, and she had ended up practically begging him to make love to her. She was a fool. Oh, she was such a weak, *stupid* fool.

'Don't look at me like that.' Suddenly he was angry, furiously angry, pulling her into a sitting position on the bed as he swore under his breath. 'You think it was easy for me to stop, is that it?' he snarled softly. 'Here—' He took her hand, holding it against his body for a shocking moment. 'Does that feel as though it was easy?'

'Don't!' She snatched her hand away, her cheeks blazing.

'You think I'm some sort of a monster—that is the truth, is it not?' he grated bitterly. 'And then you wonder why I do not want another crime laid at my feet! You don't trust me—hell, you don't even *like* me. You would have preferred me to take you like this, with things so bad between us?'

'I didn't want you to take me.' It was a lie, and not

even a very convincing one, adding tenfold to her humiliation.

'Sure.' His tone was scathing, pressing home her deceit.

'*I hate you.*'

'Do you know, I think I would prefer that to this cool disdain of the last few weeks,' he bit savagely. 'At least hate is a real emotion, one I can understand.'

There was something in his voice, a strange inflexion, that brought her head—which had been hanging down—sharply upwards to look into his face, and for a second, before the cynical mask had slid into place, she saw a dark pain that matched her own.

'Jed?' Her voice was shaking as she spoke his name.

But he was already on his feet, the metamorphosis continuing as he bent down and picked up his coat and her jacket, turning to face her with a cold, tight smile as he said, 'Shall we?' This was the Jed Cannon the world knew—ruthless, cool, inexorable— the brief glimpse of the man behind the mask a distant memory.

It helped Tamar slide off the bed slowly as she gathered the tatters of her torn dignity about her, although the effect was spoilt slightly when she had to crawl half under the bed for one shoe. She was painfully aware her hair must resemble a haystack, and that her face was almost totally devoid of its morning make-up, and this was confirmed when Jed said, his voice flat now, 'Would you like to use the bathroom before we leave?'

'Thank you.' Oh, they were being so polite, she thought with black humour as she walked into the magnificent *en suite* bathroom, locking the door behind her. She sat down with a little plop on the huge cane basket chair and shut her eyes for a full minute, before gathering herself together and walking over to one of the twin basins, peering at her reflection despairingly. Oh, she looked a sight. If this didn't put him off her, nothing would. She bit her lower lip hard, willing back the tears that were threatening to fall again by sheer determination, before reaching for her cosmetics bag and setting to.

By the time she emerged, some ten minutes later, her hair neat and tidy in its clips and her discreet make-up covering all trace of the tear-blotches and the bright red nose that had faced her a few minutes before, Tamar was in control again.

Jed was sitting waiting for her in the beautiful hall-way, and rose immediately she came into view, his dark face cool and reserved as he smiled a smile that didn't reach the metallic grey eyes. 'All ready?' She nodded without returning the smile, and he took her arm, his touch cold and impersonal.

He kept their conversation to the minimum on the drive back to the office, and when he did speak it was about the apartment and how he would like it advertised, his voice tight and clipped as he listed its advantages. Tamar listened quietly, nodding her head in all the right places as she slowly bled inside. This was awful, *awful*. How could she have been so...so *insane*? she asked herself silently. Not content with attacking him, she had then further convinced him of her instability by allowing— She closed her mind to what she had allowed. And then she had made it obvious she was piqued he hadn't followed through.

Her face began to burn again, flooding her pale cheeks with hot colour and making it difficult to sit quietly without squirming in embarrassment. He would think she needed certifying. Perhaps she *did* need certifying—

'Do you agree, Tamar?'

'What?' She came out of the morass of self-recrimination to the knowledge that Jed had been talking and she hadn't heard a word. 'I'm sorry, I didn't quite…?'

He stared at her hard for a moment, and she expected one of the cutting retorts he was so good at, but after a few seconds he shook his head slowly, his voice expressionless as he said, 'It doesn't matter. I'll ring you later this afternoon and we'll discuss details then.'

'Right.'

Once the Mercedes drew up outside Taylor and Taylor, Tamar was out of the car like a shot, without waiting for Jed to walk round and open her door, nodding at him quickly as he stood by the side of the vehicle but not stopping as she said, 'I'll talk to you later, then?' and walked across the pavement.

'Goodbye, Tamar.'

His voice was deep and rough, and the goodbye sounded terribly final, but she nodded again, keeping her tone light as she said, 'Goodbye, Jed,' and continued in to the building without turning round.

CHAPTER SEVEN

'AND that's it, then?'

Fiona couldn't have sounded more put out if it had been her own love affair that had finished, Tamar thought wryly—not that her relationship with Jed Cannon had embodied either love or an affair in its make-up. Not on his side anyway.

'Afraid so.' Tamar forced a bright smile. 'And so I'll be able to look Gaby and Olivia in the face again without any skeletons in the cupboard.'

'Blow Gaby and Olivia.' Fiona frowned at her, clicking her tongue irritably. They were standing in the tiny kitchen at the back of the building, Fiona having dragged her there after her entrance back into the office on the pretext of making some coffee. 'But why do you think he's given up, then? What happened today?'

'Nothing.' Tamar shrugged carefully. 'Nothing at all.'

It could have been Fiona's female intuition, or perhaps Tamar's beetroot-red face and faintly pink eyes had more to do with the other girl's reply of, 'And pigs might fly! Tamar, I saw his face when he was glaring at poor Tim. I thought there was going to be a riot. Now don't tell me a guy like Jed Cannon gives up the hunt without a damn good reason,' Fiona finished scathingly.

'Fi, I don't want to discuss it,' Tamar said firmly.

'All right, forget the gory details, but you must see this is a one-off opportunity, Tamar? Unattached millionaires with the sort of looks Jed Cannon has, and who fancy the pants off you to boot, don't exactly come by on every number ten bus, even for girls as gorgeous as you.'

'I mean it, Fi.' Tamar had had about as much as she could take without explaining herself to Fiona.

'It's only because I love you, you know.' Fiona suddenly looked distinctly pathetic, but Tamar had seen her use that ploy too often with Richard to be taken in. 'You've had such a rotten deal, I would love a bit of good luck to come your way.'

'*Fiona*, Jed Cannon is *not* good luck,' Tamar stated positively. 'In fact he's—'

'Before you embarrass us both by listing what I am sure was going to be a catalogue of my attributes, could I have a word?'

The completely expressionless, deep, cold voice from the small hall separating the front office from the kitchen brought both women's heads swinging round as though connected by a single wire, and if Tamar thought she had been embarrassed before, it was nothing to how she felt when she saw Jed standing in the doorway.

'Your husband assured me it was okay to come through,' Jed continued quietly, speaking directly to Fiona now, who was as red as Tamar. 'I wanted to speak to Tamar in private.'

'Oh, of course—of course.' For the first time Tamar could remember Fiona had been reduced to a gibbering idiot, but she was far too perturbed by the tall, dark man standing in front of them to dwell on her friend's lack of composure. 'I'll just go and... I'd better... I'll leave you to it,' Fiona finished weakly.

Once Fiona had scuttled away, closing the kitchen door behind her with an apologetic grimace at Tamar behind Jed's back, Tamar waited for the explosion, watching Jed warily as he walked across the small room to stare out of the window into the tiny walled yard the property boasted.

'What was the rotten deal?' His voice was soft, very soft, and so completely at odds with what she had expected that she found herself gaping at him, her mouth wide open, as he turned to face her. And it was in that moment that her love for him rose up in such an incredibly fierce flood that she had to turn her head, petrified he would read the truth in her eyes.

'Tamar?' His voice was still very soft. 'I'm not going to touch you, or make you do anything you don't want to do, but if you can tell me I'd like to know.'

'I can't.' It was a small, broken whisper, and if she had been looking at him she would have seen the dark, handsome face tighten and his eyes narrow at her distress.

There was complete silence for a moment, and then he said, slowly and distinctly, 'Okay. Well, perhaps you can answer this, then. This...antipathy—is it purely against me, or all men?'

This time the silence stretched until it was as taut as piano wire, and he had just given up all hope of her answering when she said, so softly he could barely hear, 'I...I haven't dated anyone in five years.'

He couldn't speak for a moment, a mixture of emotions tearing through his body. There was fierce relief that it wasn't him in particular she had an aversion to, but her whispered divulgence brought up a whole host of other questions, none of which he could ask. Instead he said, 'And you don't see that changing?'

She raised her head now, looking him straight in the

eyes and keeping her voice steady. 'No, I don't,' she said softly.

Over his dead body. He kept his face perfectly expressionless, nodding slowly. He could have taken her back there in the apartment, and she would have been with him every inch of the way. His body stirred, hardening at the memory. Whatever had happened, whoever this man was who had hurt her in some way and put her off the whole male sex, she had still wanted him, Jed Cannon, to make love to her. And he intended to. This thing wasn't over, not by a long chalk.

'Why…why did you come back?' Tamar asked carefully, after moments had crept by and he still didn't speak.

'You left your handbag in the car.' He had something tucked under his arm but she hadn't noticed, and now he reached out and passed her the bag.

'Oh—oh, thank you,' she stammered. 'I—I didn't realise.' Her face was hot and flushed.

'And I wanted to ask you about this weekend,' he continued smoothly. 'We didn't arrange a time for me to pick you up.'

'Pick me up…?' she repeated confusedly.

'Shall we say seven tonight? Emma and I usually eat at eight-thirty, so that will give you time to freshen up before dinner and get settled in.' He smiled at her, an open, innocent smile that didn't fool her for a minute.

'I didn't say I was coming,' she protested quickly. 'And after all that happened—' She stopped abruptly, frowning at him as he stared at her perplexedly, one eyebrow quirking in bewilderment.

'All that happened?' he repeated with suspect artlessness. 'I don't understand?'

'At...at the apartment,' she persisted nervously.

'I'm still not with you,' he said musingly. 'As far as I'm aware, nothing happened that would prevent you spending the weekend with Emma.' His voice was cool and silky soft.

Oh, she hated him. She did, she hated him. Tamar wanted to give in to the childish impulse to stamp her foot, but restrained herself, knowing it would only delight him. So, as far as Jed was concerned this morning was mere history and forgotten? He could dismiss it as easily as that? Well, it hadn't meant anything to her either. *It hadn't.* 'Fine.' Her smile was brittle. 'If I can be of help to Emma, of course I'll come.'

'That's settled, then.' It was said with such satisfaction that she realised immediately she had walked into one of Jed Cannon's traps. It was a tactic he used in business, and ruthlessly—her earlier research on him had proved that without a shadow of a doubt—and now he had applied the same cunning with her.

She glared at him, too proud to take back her words and too angry to try and pretend she was happy about the situation.

'What a little firebrand you are.' His voice was tender now, with that deep, husky timbre that made her legs weak, but she was determined he wasn't going to have it all his own way.

'Because I don't always do exactly what you say?' she asked tightly. 'Like the rest of the world?'

'A slight exaggeration, but I appreciate your faith in my sovereignty,' he said mockingly.

'You certainly act like a king with his subjects,' she fired back furiously. 'I've never known a man like you.'

'Thank you.' He bowed slightly, whilst keeping piercing silver eyes fixed on hers. 'My first compliment to date.'

'It wasn't a compliment and you know it,' she muttered angrily, knowing she wouldn't win in a war of words but unable to admit defeat. 'You're just impossible.'

'I've been called worse.' He grinned, her capitulation regarding the weekend giving a luminescence to the silver-grey eyes that was like the brilliance of a cold winter sky with the sun behind it.

'I bet,' she agreed savagely.

'Now, now, smile nicely and be respectful while we join the others,' Jed mocked softly. 'I have my reputation to think of, you know, and the rest of the world thinks I'm wonderful.'

'Huh.' It was weak, but then she'd known that razor-sharp mind was way ahead of her, Tamar seethed quietly, as Jed followed her out of the kitchen and into the office beyond.

The anger lasted all the time she watched him charm Fiona and Richard, and even bring a reluctant smile to Tim's face. Jed was putting himself out to be amusing in the same way he did everything—brilliantly—but the moment the door closed behind him, she wanted him back. Stupid, crazy, suicidal—yes, it was all of those things, Tamar admitted to herself as she sat at her desk and pretended to work, but she couldn't help it. She loved him. She only really came alive when he was around, even if most of the time they were like two gladiators in the arena.

And she should never have agreed to stay the weekend at Greenacres. The churning in her stomach increased with the thought. This was all a game to him, and no doubt he was enjoying the novelty of the chase, but it wasn't like that for her.

Jed was used to women who were quite happy to play by his rules—worldly-wise, sophisticated women, who could remain friends with him after the affair was over, perhaps even see him now and again and share a long and amorous night of passion without any sentiment for what once had been getting in the way. She bent her head over an open file and blinked back the tears that were pricking the back of her eyes; she had brought all this on herself—that was the worst thing of all to face. And now she felt like a tiny insect caught in a sticky web from which there was no escape...

The rest of the day went horribly wrong—a series of incidents meaning Tamar was galloping along Crayfield Avenue and into her house at ten to seven, with Jed arriving to pick her up at seven. She flew round the flat, stuffing clothes and her overnight things into a small suitcase, but was still in the middle of changing—without having even so much as brushed her hair—when a ring at the doorbell downstairs heralded his arrival.

She pulled on a pair of grey leggings, followed by a mid-thigh-length ivory cashmere jumper she meant to team with matching boots, but was still in bare feet, her hair a mass of riotous red-gold curls about her shoulders, when there was a knock at her front door.

'Darn it.' She glanced desperately round the chaotic disorder of her bedroom and then, when the imperious summons sounded again, sighed irritably. She'd just have to let him in and get him to wait until she was ready. But she hadn't wanted him in her home. Until now she had always been waiting for his car, to avoid just this situation. It was silly, but she hadn't wanted to be able to picture him in the flat once he was out of her life for good—as he soon would be—and also her home was part of *her*. She had painted the walls, chosen the furniture, designed and had installed the tiny kitchen— her home said a lot about her, and she hadn't wanted it exposed to that shrewd, formidably intelligent mind. It made her feel too vulnerable.

She shut the bedroom door quickly and padded along to the front door, aware of her dishevelment but not having the time to do anything about it.

'Hi.'

A bolt of electricity caused every cell and nerve-ending to jump as she opened the door and saw Jed standing there. He was more casually dressed than she had ever seen him before, the black jeans and heavy black leather jacket emphasising his dark, alien attractiveness and formidable height, and causing her stomach muscles to curl and contract.

'Hallo.' Her smile was nervous. 'I'm sorry, I'm not quite ready. There was panic after panic at work this afternoon.'

He nodded lazily. 'Do you want me to wait in the car?' he asked softly.

He knew. He *knew* she didn't want him inside the flat, Tamar thought weakly. She opened her mouth to say yes, but instead found herself saying, 'No, of course not. Come in a moment. I won't be long,' as she stepped back from the doorway.

Immediately he stepped into her tiny hall the flat seemed to shrink in size, his powerfully compelling aura strong and virile in her little home. He seemed even more dangerous, even more threatening than normal, Tamar thought weakly, his dark magnetism of a type that caused little shivers of awareness to flicker up and down her spine.

'What is it?'

She must have been staring at him, because his voice was faintly surprised when he spoke, although there was a lazy, mocking quality that intimated he knew how wary she was.

'Nothing.' She smiled brightly, waving him through to the beautiful little red and gold sitting room that was the essence of the flat. She hadn't quibbled about the expense of anything for this room; she had wanted an atmosphere of beauty and peace and light, and the exquisite little room, with its tiny balcony festooned with pots of Japanese anemones, Michaelmas daisies, dwarf salvias and bright golden-yellow coneflowers, was a rebellion against the difficult, soul-searing days at university. 'I won't be long,' she said breathlessly, indicating for him to be seated on the handsome little Victorian sofa as she spoke.

He didn't move from the middle of the room, where he had come to a halt, remaining quite still for a long moment before he turned to look at her in the open doorway. 'This is quite beautiful, Tamar,' he said, with a deep, appreciative softness that stroked at her overwrought nerves.

'Thank you.' She was surprised how much it mattered. She had told him the bare outline of her childhood—her parents' death and subsequent upbringing with her aunt and family—over Sunday lunch at the quaint little pub some weeks ago, so now she added simply, 'I wanted something that was all mine.'

'I can understand that.' He smiled, and she felt the need to escape to the privacy of her bedroom and compose herself before she committed the unforgivable mistake of flinging herself wholesale into his arms. But he just looked so utterly, overwhelmingly *gorgeous*, and she loved him so much.

'I...I won't be long,' she said again, her voice breathless.

'Don't worry, I can be patient when I have to be,' he murmured with silky intent, his silver eyes piercing her defences.

Tamar looked at him in something of a daze before she nodded quickly and backed into the hall, shutting the door firmly behind her. Oh, he was dangerous. He was so, so dangerous. And she had virtually put her head in the lion's mouth, she thought despairingly. Well, it was too late now. Much, much too late—on several counts.

Jed said very little on the drive to Greenacres, which was just as well. Tamar was having enough difficulty in co-ordinating her breathing in the close confines of the Ferrari, without having to worry about making coherent conversation as well, and she was petrified the trembling in her body would communicate itself to her voice if she tried to talk. And he would love that boost to his ego, she thought despairingly—knowing that he had reduced her to a shivering wreck.

Emma was waiting for them when Jed ushered Tamar into the elegant drawing room at Greenacres, and the other girl's pale, drawn face brought an immediate surge of compassion, mingled with guilt, into Tamar's chest.

This must be a terrible time for Emma, Tamar thought sympathetically, bending over the wheelchair and hugging Jed's sister before she sat down herself. With the moment of truth regarding the pioneer treatment approaching fast, the breakdown of her marriage and the sale of her home, added to the often unpleasant side effects the drugs induced, she must be reaching the end of her tether.

Jed had confided that most of his sister's friends had fallen by the wayside due to Ronald Mitchell's manipulative control over his wife, and that Emma's youthful aspirations for a career in medicine had been put on hold—along with her life, it seemed—on her marriage. What havoc men could cause. The thought tightened Tamar's soft lips, and she had to make a conscious effort with her voice as she said, 'It's so nice to see you again, Emma. I missed you the last time I was here.'

'I'll leave Emma to settle you in,' Jed put in smoothly, 'if you don't mind. I've one or two urgent calls to make, and there's a fax in my study that needs examining.'

'Go on, go on.' Emma was smiling up at her brother and, like before, Tamar was touched by the love and understanding between the two siblings. 'He never stops working,' Emma continued as Jed turned to leave. 'I'm sure that fax goes to bed with him most nights.'

'I don't get any better offers these days.' It was flung over his shoulder as he opened the door, but he didn't look back, for which Tamar was eternally grateful, hot colour flooding her face until her cheeks burnt.

Why did he have to reduce everything to that one basic desire? Tamar asked herself silently as she made small talk with Emma. But she knew why. This powerfully emotive feeling between them, heightened by love on her side and sheer old-fashioned lust on his, was all-consuming. In the last few weeks it was in every sunset that blazed across the night sky, every melodious bird song, even the fine tracery of a glittering spider's web covered with dew that she had seen on her way to work that morning. She couldn't escape him. She would never be able to escape him...

By the time Jed came to take the two women through to dinner, some forty minutes later, Emma had confided most of her deepest anxieties to Tamar, a fact she only seemed to become aware of as her brother strolled into the room.

'Oh, I'm sorry, I've done nothing but talk about me,' Emma said quickly as she looked at Tamar with puppy-dog sad eyes. 'I'm not normally like this—in fact I find it difficult to talk to people at all—but you're different.'

'Isn't she?' Jed agreed softly, his voice deep and slumberous as he looked down on the mass of red and gold curls.

Tamar searched for something light to say, but lucid thought evaded her, mainly because of the lean, masculine body just inches away. He had discarded the leather jacket on entering the house, and his black silk shirt, open at the neck and with slightly gathered sleeves, emphasised the broad shoulders and muscled chest more than if he had been naked. *Naked*... Tamar flushed violently and jumped to her feet like a spring, causing both Jed and Emma some surprise. 'I'm starving.' Her voice was too shrill, and she tried to cover the fact with a bright smile.

'Then the reputable Mrs Trotter has the perfect remedy,' Jed said smoothly, allowing Emma to precede them in her motorised chair. 'If it's food you're referring to,' he added softly, when his sister was out of earshot. 'Otherwise, I'd be glad to personally satisfy your appetite...'

'In your dreams,' she snapped back sharply, hating him, loving him. 'Satisfy your appetite'. That was all making love with her would mean to him—an animal need sated, she told herself bitterly. And she'd known it from day one, so it shouldn't hurt so much.

'Ah, now, my dreams.' He seemed quite unmoved by her ill-humour. 'Remind me to tell you about my dreams some time,' he murmured lazily, taking her arm as he spoke.

'Your dreams are nothing to do with me,' Tamar said cuttingly.

'Tamar, my dreams are *everything* to do with you.' He folded her into him as they walked through to the dining room after Emma, his arm a band of steel round her waist, and she found she couldn't argue with him any more. Not with his thigh against hers and the faint seductive smell of him teasing her nostrils and inflaming her senses.

Dinner was a delicious affair of five courses, and by the time coffee was served by the beaming Mrs Trotter, who was well pleased with Tamar's enthusing over the meal, Tamar was full to bursting.

'Do you always eat like this?' she asked Jed in astonishment, her gaze moving innocently over his lean frame.

'Always,' he assured her solemnly, only relaxing into an amused smile when Emma protested.

'Don't believe him, Tamar. Unless we have guests for dinner, Jed lets Mrs Trotter have the evenings to herself. She either prepares something for us earlier, or Jed cooks us a meal.'

'You?' Tamar couldn't have looked more astonished if he had suddenly sprouted horns and a forked tail, and his quirked eyebrows reflected his acknowledgement of her amazement when he murmured, 'Monsters shouldn't be able to cook, eh?'

'Monsters!' Emma laughed lightly, totally oblivious to any undercurrents. 'You're the most unmonster-like person I've ever met. Impatient, maybe, untidy, definitely, and the worst perfectionist I've ever come across in my life, but you're as soft as marshmallow on the inside. Don't you think so, Tamar?'

Tamar was completely taken aback, and it showed in her half-open mouth and blank eyes as she stared at Jed's sister, utterly lost for words.

How long she would have continued to sit there in mute helplessness if Jed hadn't taken pity on her she didn't know, but when he smiled lazily, and said, 'Oh, Tamar is my greatest admirer, Emma,' his sister nodded happily, before applying herself to her cheese and biscuits, clearly having received the answer she expected.

'Tamar is my greatest admirer'. Tamar stared at the dark, mocking face across the table for a long moment before smiling carefully and taking a sip of coffee, aiming to appear composed and unruffled. The cynical undertone had been for her ears alone, which made his words even more ironic, she thought bitterly. If he did but know, he was dangerously on track.

Once they had finished coffee, Emma immediately announced her intention of going to bed. Jed's sister had been yawning on and off all through dinner, and it was clear she was tired, but Tamar suspected Emma was trying to be tactful too. Jed hadn't told her how he had explained her weekend visit to his sister, and she hadn't asked, but she sensed Emma thought they were romantically involved—which was logical after all.

Did Emma know her brother's views on love and marriage? Tamar asked herself thoughtfully, as she watched Jed rise and kiss the top of Emma's head as he wished her goodnight. She doubted it. She doubted it very much. And as for being as soft as marshmallow... She wrinkled her nose against such foolishness.

'Brandy?' Jed offered once they were alone. 'Or how about another coffee? Or even a combination of the two? I do a mean liqueur, with one or two spices and whipped cream.'

Tamar's eyes widened appreciatively, and, seeing her expression, Jed stood up, walking round the table and taking her hand as he said, 'Come on, you can come and watch me while I perform a minor miracle. Mrs Trotter has gone to bed now, so we won't get in her way,' his voice soft and teasing.

This was too cosy, too intimate. The warning was there as she walked through to the huge, beautifully fitted kitchen hand in hand with him, but, once in Mrs Trotter's immaculate domain, Jed made no effort to follow up on the brief contact.

'Sit yourself there and watch a genius at work.' He indicated one of the tall breakfast stools grouped round a large circular breakfast bar in the middle of the room, and Tamar clambered up obediently, feeling both relieved and bereft at the same time.

The coffee was absolutely delicious, and after her first sip, when her blissful expression as she inhaled the fragrant liquid spoke for itself, Jed joined her with his own cup. 'Nice, eh?' he said easily, his voice warm.

'It's lovely.' Her pink tongue came out to lick a drop of foam off her lips, and his body responded with muscle-clenching swiftness. 'Really lovely. And you cook too?'

'When the mood takes me.' He smiled at her with narrowed silver eyes, his lazy air and apparent relaxed demeanour lulling her into a state of false security. The three glasses of wine she had imbibed during the meal, added to the hefty measure of brandy in the coffee, helped too.

'Who taught you? Your mother?' she asked quietly.

'No, not my mother.'

He hadn't moved a muscle, and the dark, handsome face was just the same as it had been a moment before she spoke, but something had changed. She felt it deep in the heart of her, in the secret place where her love for him resided. And, with the alcohol loosening her tongue, she persisted, 'Didn't your mother like cooking, or was she too busy, perhaps? My aunt always was.'

'My mother—' He stopped abruptly, and Tamar could almost see the razor-sharp brain ticking over and deciding whether to continue, before he said, his tone flat now, 'My mother was a beautiful butterfly, Tamar. A beautiful, enchanting, immoral butterfly.' He stared at her, the silver eyes like transparent ice.

'Immoral?' She stared at him, frightened by the darkness in his face. He couldn't be saying his own mother had been immoral, surely?

'She was born into a poor American family in the deep South, and she was determined to get out the minute she could. At sixteen she left for the big city, and was working there when my father saw her outside a store one day when he was over in the States on holiday. It was love at first sight for him, and he continued to love her right up until the day he died.'

'And your mother?' Tamar asked softly. 'Did she fall in love with him at once?'

'My father was forty to her eighteen when they met,' Jed said bitterly, 'and he seemed very, very rich to a little girl from the cotton plantations. She knew he would look after her.'

'Are you saying she didn't love him?' Tamar asked uncertainly.

'She didn't love anyone but herself.' He smiled mirthlessly. 'I think my father lost count of her lovers over the years.'

'And your father didn't mind?' Her voice was incredulous, betraying her shock.

'He minded, but...he loved her. They used to row all the time. Emma and I were brought up on screaming fights and long, cold silences. But at bottom he preferred to be miserable with her than miserable without her, I guess. I've never been able to understand why.' His voice carried a note of genuine puzzlement. 'She was a lousy wife and a lousy mother—none of us got any affection, although my dad used to try and make up for the love and attention she didn't give us. He was great; warm, loving, a real nice guy.' He shook his head slowly, his eyes bleak.

'Do you know, she actually turned up at his funeral with a male escort young enough to be her son? Although to be fair she looked as young as him. She was incredibly beautiful...'

'Oh, Jed.' She didn't know what to say or how to say it.

'And then two years later she was dead, and even that was messy. She and the latest boyfriend went swimming in the Caribbean one night when they were high on something and drowned. Poetic justice, really—she'd been waiting for my father to kick the bucket for years, but she didn't get as long as she'd expected to enjoy the results of her whoring,' he finished bitterly.

'Her whoring?' Tamar repeated in horror.

'What else do you call it when you sleep with someone for money? That's what she did from the first day she met him.'

He was so angry, so cold, so bitter. She couldn't defend how his mother had behaved, but Tamar said gently, 'But she had you and Emma. At least she gave your father a son and a daughter. You must have been a comfort to him.'

'A son and a daughter.' The way he said it made her blood run cold, and then he turned to look at her, his rigid body stiff with pain. 'Tamar, just after my mother was drowned, Emma developed the bone disease,' he said with a terrible lack of expression. 'Necessary tests proved Emma was the natural child of my mother and father, and I was not.'

'What?' She heard the words but couldn't take them in. 'I don't understand.'

'It's simple,' he said harshly. 'My mother got pregnant by one of her lovers. I was not my father's son.'

She wanted to say something to take away the devastating pain evident in his face, something that would remove the tortured blackness from his eyes, but she couldn't think of a single word. She simply stared at him as her eyes filled with tears, biting on her lower lip to stop its quivering.

'It's all right. It's all right.' Now he was comforting her, his voice deep and soft and tender. 'It's all history, Tamar.' He stood up, pulling her into him, and she went blindly, resting her cheek against the soft silk of his shirt as he continued, 'The worst thing was imagining my father knew I wasn't his flesh and blood, but I don't think he could have done. Certainly Emma doesn't think so. He always treated us exactly the same, loved us the same.'

'He *was* your father, in every way that mattered,' Tamar said with muffled urgency, her nose buried in his chest as he rested his chin in the silk of her hair. 'He brought you up, became both father and mother in the bad times and the good.'

'I know.' His voice was very husky. 'But I wanted to belong to him by blood. I couldn't believe my mother had been so cruel. I suppose the sense of betrayal was heightened by the fact that I had caught the girl I was engaged to in the arms of a friend of mine a few weeks before my mother's accident. I began to think the world was rotten from the inside out.'

'Or the female part of it,' she murmured softly, drawing away a little and raising her head to look into the dark face above hers. This explained so much. She didn't want to know, not really, and yet she couldn't bear not knowing, and so she asked, 'This girl, your fiancée? What happened after you found out?'

'I left.' It was very cold and very simple.

He had been engaged once. He had asked someone to share the rest of her life with him. The stab of jealousy was unworthy of her, she knew that, but she couldn't help it. And this girl must have been mad, crazy, to throw away a lifetime of loving with such a man. Did she know what she had done, along with this woman who had been his mother and sounded the most unnatural parent in the world?

Tamar wanted to ask a thousand questions, but she knew not one of them could be voiced. He was a lonely man; she could see that now. He might have his women, along with fabulous wealth and a glittering career, but the cynicism caused by a troubled childhood in an unhappy home with warring parents, followed by his fiancée's betrayal and then the shock of finding out about his parentage, had cut deep, bitter wounds in his psyche that perhaps could never be healed. She could understand where his sceptical, scornful attitude to marriage and love came from after all that he had endured—understand it, but not acquiesce to it.

She didn't want to cry—she knew he was the type of man who would find even the merest trace of pity distasteful if it was directed at him—but her eyes were blurred as she said, 'Thank your for telling me.'

'I didn't intend to.' There was a note of surprise in the husky voice. 'I've never discussed all this with anyone before, but, like Emma said, you're different.'

But not different enough. She blinked her eyes furiously, staring up at him as she tried to control her feelings. But he must have seen something in the wounded doe-brown eyes, because the hard, handsome face softened and he groaned deep in his throat, his mouth moving hungrily over hers.

The kiss was one of fierce passion that sent the blood rushing through her body like warm mulled wine, and she was powerless to resist the intoxication of it, abandoning herself to his hands and mouth with a completeness that would have shocked her if she had been aware of it. But she was lost in mindless emotion, the pounding of his heart, the small sounds he was making at the back of his throat as his hands and mouth continued to caress her, taking her to another dimension.

She could feel his hands on her bare skin, but the gentle eroticism was neither rough or threatening, and she began to tremble with the sweetness of it. For years the thought of a man's passion had been something alien and frightening, but this was pure pleasure, and she twisted languorously in his arms, murmuring incoherently as her fingers felt the tremors that rippled across the hard male body, the thick muscles in his shoulders bunched under her hands.

His thighs were close against hers, and his hand in the small of her back urged her even closer, until she could feel every inch of him. She wanted him, she needed him, Tamar thought frantically, pressing herself into him in a primitive invitation she would have been amazed at only minutes earlier. And then she felt him stiffen, his hands and mouth freezing for a second before he pushed her from him and said, his voice broken and urgent, 'Emma,' moments before Tamar heard the wheelchair in the hall outside.

She just had time to hastily adjust her rumpled clothing before she slid onto the stool she had vacated. Jed tucked his shirt into the waistband of his jeans at the same time, and then moved to stand by the coffee machine, before the door opened and Jed's sister came in.

'Hallo, again.' If Emma noticed Tamar's wildly flushed cheeks and tousled hair she gave no indication of it, smiling blithely at her brother as she said, 'I couldn't sleep, so I thought I'd do myself some hot milk. But if that's one of your famous coffees…?'

In direct contrast to her breathless state, Tamar noticed Jed was his normal cool, controlled self when he answered briefly, 'Coffee won't help you sleep,' his voice expressionless.

'I know,' Emma said regretfully. 'Okay, I'll fix myself some milk—although that coffee smells heavenly.'

'It tastes it too.' Tamar forced herself to enter the conversation with a light smile, praying that the burning embarrassment she was feeling wasn't evident to either of them. 'But I'm bushed. Today was one of those days when it would have been better not to get out of bed, so if you don't mind I'll go up to my room now.'

She drained the last of the coffee as she finished speaking, standing up and nodding at them both as she said, 'Goodnight, then, sleep well.'

Jed's reply was a sardonically raised eyebrow and a rueful shake of his head. 'Somehow I don't think that's an option tonight,' he said expressionlessly. 'I think I might do a few lengths of the pool before I turn in, and burn off some excess...energy.'

Tamar managed to get out of the kitchen without disgracing herself, and fairly flew up to her room on the second floor of the house which had a panoramic view over half of Windsor. Once she had shut the door behind her she leant against it for long, calming minutes, her eyes shut and her breast heaving as she fought for control, and then she opened her eyes slowly before switching on the light and walking across to the big double bed.

It was a beautiful room... She gazed weakly at her surroundings as she collapsed on the bed. Most of her flat could fit into this space, and the shades of aqua-blues and greens, combined with the lime-green and yellow that were reflected in the curtains, carpet and bed furniture, and the small cane suite in the far corner of the room by the window, could only have been put together by an expert.

She hadn't had time to take much in when Emma had shown her her room during their pre-dinner chat, but she remembered the *ensuite* bathroom was in pale green marble, and that— again—it could swallow half her flat whole, and the walk-in wardrobe was of a size to get lost in. All this wealth and power... She shivered suddenly, but the chill was from within, not without.

Tamar sat for a long, long time in the soft, muted lighting, her mind dissecting every word, every glance, every touch she and Jed had shared, and by the time she rose to run herself a bath in the enormous tub she had come to a decision. Several decisions, in fact, she told herself grimly.

She had to come clean about how she had inveigled herself into his life in the first place, and explain her less than honourable motives. He might understand—he might not. Her heart turned over and she took a deep breath to stop the panic taking hold. She would tell him about Gaby and Ronald—all of it. She owed him that at least. And she would explain something she had only just realised herself, this very night. In seeking him out as she had, in trying to play him at his own game, she had been aiming at retribution for what Mike Goodfellow had put her through. It hadn't just been Gaby she had sought to avenge, but herself...

The tears were hot and salty on her face as she slid into the warm water, silky with fragrant bubbles, but still her thoughts went on.

In explaining the reasons for her appearance in his life she would have to tell him about the rape—that would be hard. She shuddered, shutting her eyes tight for a moment as her heart pounded. She had no idea how a proud, commanding man like him would react. It could be with distaste, pity, disgust—he might even secretly blame her, thinking she had enticed her lecturer to act as he'd done. Certainly his view of women couldn't be any lower...

She sat up abruptly, reaching for the expensive bottle of shampoo that was grouped with many other pots of bath oils and skin and hair care lotions at the side of the bath, and, after pouring a liberal amount into the palm of her hand, began to wash her hair vigorously, her mind racing as she considered her options.

However Jed reacted, she had to tell him. The knowledge caused her to become still for a moment. After all he had confided, the honesty with which he had spoken, she had to tell him the truth without any holds barred. She just couldn't do anything else.

The foam was dripping down into her eyes, and she rinsed her thick mass of hair quickly before relaxing in the warm water again. And she had to tell him she couldn't cope with a casual affair—that she understood why he thought the way he did, but that it would kill her to sleep with him knowing he would be gone in a month or two, a year or two—whatever. She wanted a lifetime commitment with the next man who took her body, because, made as she was, she knew he would be taking her mind too. And if Jed still didn't accept that, still tried to persuade her to go to bed with him, then in the last resort she would confess that she loved him. That would be enough to scare him away for good, Tamar thought with grim self-derision.

The water was cooling by the time she padded through into the bedroom wrapped in a big fluffy towelling robe, and she sat for some time drying her hair, her mind aching with the exhaustion of going round and round in circles.

She wasn't in Jed Cannon's league; she never had been. He was a highly discriminating man, as well as being a clever and ruthless one. What did she know about keeping such a male interested? she asked herself flatly, sliding under the thick, flower-scented linen covers with a deep, trembling sigh.

She would tell him first thing in the morning, after breakfast, and then, if he still wanted her to stay for the weekend to be company for Emma, she would make sure she wasn't alone with him for the rest of her visit. Of course he might pack her off home immediately... She stared despairingly across the room, her eyes desolate as she relived the wretched sound of his voice when he had told her about his mother and fiancée, and then she reached for the little primrose-yellow lamp at the side of the bed and clicked it off, only to lie wide awake in the warm darkness for hours.

CHAPTER EIGHT

IN SPITE of only falling asleep in the early-morning hours, Tamar was awake long before dawn, and she rose from the crumpled bed, where she had tossed and turned and agonised, to sit by the window in one of the cushioned cane chairs.

Dawn came slowly, creeping across the charcoal night sky with tentative blue and pink fingers and causing a medley of birdsong in the garden below.

She was terrified at the prospect of admitting to Jed that she had set out to fool him, she acknowledged dully, but more than that, *more than that*, it was telling him about Mike Goodfellow's attack that was swamping her in black misery and paralysing her throat. But perhaps she wouldn't have to go that far anyway? Maybe once she had said her piece about Gaby he would be glad to see the back of her. That thought held no comfort whatsoever.

She had never once talked about the assault. The blue and pink rivulets in the sky above were edged with silver now—the silver of Jed's eyes. She just hadn't been able to, somehow. It had been referred to at times, obliquely, carefully, by stalwart friends like Fiona, and Gaby, and those close to her, but, apart from the cold-blooded facts for the police and her testimony in court, she hadn't shared her anguish at the pain and degradation with anyone. She had known she couldn't speak about it without losing control, and since the night of the attack control had become all-important. But now, suddenly, her feelings had gone haywire, and it was all due to one man, with silver-grey eyes and a smile to die for.

She rose restlessly, standing with her arms wrapped round her waist as she hugged herself tightly and looked out into the sleeping garden. It was quite light now...

Tamar left her room just before nine for breakfast, and had reached the hall when Emma called to her from the small hydraulic lift Jed had had installed in the stairwell of the big winding staircase. Tamar waited until the lift had reached the hall and the other girl had wheeled herself out, and they were both making their way towards the dining room when the doorbell rang.

'It'll be the postman,' Emma said knowingly as Tamar turned on her heel and went to the front door. 'Jed often has the odd package or two delivered.'

It wasn't the postman. It was a tall, good-looking man with raven-black hair and deep blue eyes. Hard, cold deep blue eyes.

'Hallo.' He smiled, his eyes sweeping up and down her body with frank appreciation, and Tamar knew instantly she didn't like him. 'Is Emma up yet?' he asked, with some presumption.

'Emma?' Tamar asked warily. 'Who shall I say wants her?'

'Her husband,' Ronald Mitchell answered arrogantly.

Tamar heard a soft gasp behind her, and she hoped it hadn't reached the ears of Ronald, who was still smiling with a confidently cool composure that confirmed every thought she had ever had about this man. 'I'm sorry.' Tamar's face was straight and her voice verging on icy as Emma's husband made a movement with his body to indicate he expected her to stand aside and allow him entrance. 'I wasn't aware Emma was expecting you?'

'That's my and Emma's business, surely?' He wasn't smiling any longer.

'Not exactly.' Tamar stood her ground, holding onto the door tightly and even closing it an inch or two. 'She is living with her brother now, and so that makes it his business too.'

'Ah, I see.' The sapphire eyes narrowed and his mouth curled with contempt. 'I thought you might be a friend of Emma's, but you're one of Jed's women, aren't you? Well, don't take too much on yourself, sweetheart, because the great man doesn't like any claims on his freedom, and you're only one in a long, long line that's come and gone since I've been around. Now, as I presume Jed isn't here—'

'Why would you presume that, Mitchell?'

Tamar hadn't been aware of Jed leaving his study and walking with panther-like swiftness to the door, but now, as he gently moved her to one side and came fully into the doorway, Tamar saw the other man hastily back away a step or two, his face blanching.

'Jed.' Ronald tried to recover and force a smile, but Jed's deadly gaze froze it midway. 'You're always in the office before eight on a Saturday, I just thought...'

'Don't think, Mitchell, just get the hell out of here before I do what I've been itching to do for years,' Jed said grimly.

'I want to talk to Emma.' The cool arrogance had all gone.

'*Over my dead body.*' It had the force of a pistol-shot.

Tamar could see Emma hadn't moved from her position at the side of the hall, and that the other girl had

her fists to her mouth and a look of sheer fright on her
face. It was clear the last person in all the world that
Emma wanted to see was Ronald Mitchell. Tamar didn't
blame her.

'This is a personal matter—'

'There are no personal matters between you and my
sister anymore. You had one woman too many and she's
had enough—and, like I said when I had you escorted
from my office building, you're finished,' Jed said with
biting acidity.

'We're still man and wife.' There was a definite whine
to the other man's voice now. 'I've been worried about
her.'

'Worried?' Jed snarled scathingly. 'Spare me the soft
soap, Mitchell. I know exactly why you've come sniffing
round this morning. Your lady-friend has seen the light
and given you the elbow, hasn't she? And don't bother
to deny it. I know all about you, and I'm aware of every
move you make before you make it. She got tired of
paying all the bills, didn't she? Once I'd given you the
sack. You're slipping, Mitchell.' And now the grating
voice was lethal. 'You're getting older; you're losing
your touch.'

'You've put the word out, haven't you?' Ronald was
as white as a sheet, but Tamar didn't feel the slightest
shred of sympathy for him—she just hoped Jed didn't
lose his temper and hit the other man. Ronald would
milk a court case for all it was worth. 'Every door is
closed to me.'

'You'll have me crying in a minute.' The contempt
was biting.

'I'm warning you—'

And then Ronald stopped abruptly, his eyes widening

in terror as Jed growled, '*You're* warning *me*?' and he moved back so quickly as Jed took a step forward that he slipped, sprawling on the drive in an undignified tangle of limbs and then hotching away on his bottom as Jed continued to move towards him.

'Jed! Jed, don't.' Tamar found herself clutching hold of Jed's arm in an effort to stop him. 'It's not worth it, don't you see? You don't want the police involved—think of Emma.'

'Stay out of this, Tamar.' Jed tried to shake her off as he followed the cringing figure in front of them. 'He's had this coming.'

'Tamar?' Ronald had stopped his slithering, seemingly arrested at the sound of her name. 'There can't be too many women with that name. What's going on? Why is she here?'

Oh, no. Gaby had talked about her. But of course Gaby would talk about her. They'd always been so close, so very much like sisters it would have been natural for Gaby to discuss her family. She had thought this was the man she was going to marry, after all, the man she had willingly and happily given her virginity to. The man who had broken her heart.

'Don't try to get out of it, Mitchell,' Jed growled furiously as he reached the other man and stood glaring down at him. 'At least *act* like a man.' But Ronald was transfixed by Tamar.

'What was the other name? Oh, yes, McKinley. *Tamar McKinley*. I have it now. I thought I recognised you when you opened the door, but I didn't connect you with Gabrielle,' Ronald said slowly, his eyes narrowing into blue slits of glass. 'But then I'd only seen a photo.'

'What is this?' Ronald's obvious bewilderment and

his mention of Gaby's name had pierced Jed's blind rage, and he turned to Tamar with an irritable frown. 'Do you know Gabrielle Connolly?'

She hadn't wanted it to be like this. Tamar was conscious of a deep, mortifying sense of guilt. She had wanted to tell him herself, quietly, unemotionally, but now that option was gone. And he would never believe she had meant to confess all that very morning.

She was right; he didn't.

'Yes, I know Gaby,' Tamar said tremblingly, the quiver in her voice causing Jed's eyes to search her pale face. 'She...she's my cousin,' she admitted quietly.

'Your cousin?' He stared at her, the man at his feet seemingly forgotten. 'Not one of the cousins you were brought up with?'

'Yes.' It was very small, a mere whisper, but it seemed to fire something in the dark face as Jed said, 'You knew? About your cousin and him?' And he gestured contemptuously at Ronald, who had now struggled to his feet. 'Why didn't you say something?'

'I...' She shook her head helplessly, unable to go on with Ronald standing there. 'I can explain.'

'I bet you can.' Ronald's voice was blustering, but it was clear he still couldn't make head or tail of the twist in the situation when he said, 'Don't think you fool me, Jed. You've got her here as some sort of witness against me, haven't you? Poisoning Emma's mind against me—'

'*Shut up.*' The words were soft but held such menace Ronald did shut up, continuing to back slowly away down the drive without taking his eyes off Jed's face. But Jed wasn't looking at his brother-in-law. He was looking at Tamar, and she shrank from what she read in his face.

'Get in the house.'

Just four little words, but they chilled Tamar to the bone. 'Jed, please, I was going to tell you—'

'Get in the house,' he repeated, with a curious lack of expression that was worse than any raging.

Ronald had seized the opportunity to escape, and was now running down the drive in a frantic gallop, but neither Tamar or Jed noticed him as Tamar nodded slowly, turning in one helpless, defeated movement and walking ahead of Jed into the house.

Emma was waiting in the hall, her face still chalk-white but her eyes hopeful as she said, 'He's gone? Ronald's gone?'

Jed nodded, his voice clipped and his face blank when he said, 'I need to talk to Tamar alone, Emma. Go and have your breakfast and don't worry about Ronald. It's finished.'

And so were they. She could read it in the white-hot rage that had turned the beautiful eyes into slits of razor-sharp steel. He would never understand now, whatever she said. His treatment at the hands of the women who had given birth to him, the lack of love from the female half of his parents—the supposedly softer, gentler side—had been bad enough, but when added to his fiancée's betrayal, and then the revelation that because of his mother's loose living the one person he had loved, respected, adored, was no relation at all, it killed any chance she might have had at reaching him stone-dead. He would hate her—he *did* hate her; she could read it in his face.

'My study.' He pointed down the hall and Tamar

walked down it, aware of Emma's surprised, questioning eyes on her face as she passed the other girl, but not daring to speak.

'Well?' Jed had shut the door behind him, and they now stood in the middle of the large book-lined room, the littered desk and a busy fax machine indicating he had been at work before Ronald's intrusion. 'You said you could explain, so explain,' he said with tight control.

'It's true that Gaby is my cousin, and…and that I planned to get to know you,' Tamar said feverishly, her colour coming and going in a face that was like lint. 'I was going to tell you this morning—I was really. After…after last night.'

'When I made such a fool of myself, you mean,' he said coldly, 'and told you the story of my life. Go on.'

'When you went to see Ronald and Gaby, when they were having dinner at the hotel—you remember?'

She paused and he nodded savagely, saying, 'In their love-nest, yes, I remember,' and then waiting for her to continue.

'Well, she had no idea that Ronald was married, none at all. And…and she was pregnant by him.'

'*What?*' He stared at her. 'I don't believe it.'

'It's true.' She swallowed deeply and forced herself to go on. 'She…she hadn't been with anyone before Ronald—Gaby's not like that—and she thought he loved her, that he wanted to marry her. It came as a shock, a terrible shock, to find out in the way she did, and with everyone listening.'

'She deserved it; she had been sleeping with my sister's husband—'

'She didn't *know*,' Tamar said heatedly. 'She didn't. Ronald charmed her and wheedled his way into her affections, and before she knew where she was...' She shrugged painfully.

'What are you going to tell me now? That there's a little Ronald out there somewhere?' he asked caustically.

'No.' He was looking at her as though he had never seen her before, as though he loathed and despised her. 'No,' she repeated slowly. 'Gaby lost the baby—the night you confronted them both in the hotel.'

'And you consider that my fault?' he asked grimly.

'She...she tried to commit suicide that night,' Tamar said wretchedly, hearing his sudden intake of breath with a pain that sliced her through. 'She lived, but the baby didn't.'

'And your appearance in my office that day—you'd planned that?' he asked with condemning clarity. 'What was the idea? To get me interested and then dump me, like Ronald dumped Gaby? Or were you going to try something more, make a public spectacle of me, something along those lines?'

'No. Yes. Oh, I don't know,' she blurted desperately. 'I wanted to make you understand what Gaby had gone through, how it *felt*.' She stared at him helplessly, her head whirling.

'I see.' Dark colour had flared across the chiselled cheekbones and his eyes were the colour of granite. 'So it was all a game, right from the start—a game of revenge. You hated me and you wanted to hurt me, so you manipulated me and the situation.' He took a long, rasping breath before he snarled, 'How the pair of you must have laughed when I began to chase you, and last night must have been the icing on the cake.'

'No, Gaby doesn't know I've been seeing you,' Tamar said wretchedly. 'It's not like that. I promise you—'

'You *promise* me?' he ground out through clenched teeth. 'Well, excuse me if that doesn't carry too much weight right now. And I thought you were so gentle, so nervous, so *different*. Damn it, you're different, all right. I thought I'd seen it all, Tamar, but you sure as hell take the biscuit.'

'Jed, please—please.' She couldn't bear this; she couldn't go through this and survive it. 'Listen to me.'

'And the "Don't touch me, I'm as pure as the driven snow" routine was cute,' he said bitterly, self-disgust in his voice when he went on, 'You sure took me in with that. I thought you were shy, vulnerable; I've been going half-crazy trying to go slowly, so as not to shock your moral sensibilities. Moral sensibilities!' He gave a harsh bark of a laugh. 'Lady, you're a winner—a twenty-four-carat winner. You even had the foresight to admit you'd already slept with a man so I didn't get suspicious when you finally allowed me to make love to you. And you would have, wouldn't you?' he said contemptuously. 'If it meant you could make me look more of a fool when you slapped me in the face with all this.'

'It wasn't like that.' She wanted to cry and shout and scream, but she knew she had to remain calm and make him *see*. 'I was telling you the truth when I said I hadn't dated for so long. You see, something happened at university—'

'Spare me more of your lies,' he spat savagely, his revulsion freezing her throat and strangling anything more she might have said. 'You played me perfectly, Tamar. I see it all now. The slightest bit of encouragement at the start, then a retreat, then a bit more giving. What was the theory—give a wolf a taste and he'll be

back for more? Well, it worked. You must be feeling
very pleased with yourself right now.'

'Please listen to me—'

'I don't want to listen to you, Tamar. I don't want to
even look at you,' he said bitterly. 'Did Emma feature
in this plan of yours? Did you intend to try and get at
her too?'

'No!' she exclaimed desperately, and then, more
calmly, 'No, no. You must believe me.'

'"Must" doesn't come into it,' he said grimly. 'But I
tell you one thing, Tamar—you try and hurt my sister
and you'll regret it until the day you die.'

She couldn't believe he was saying these things to her,
that he was thinking about her in this way. But she deserved it, she thought wildly. She deserved everything
he could say or think. And his reaction proved what she
had known all along—he had never really cared for her
as a *person*. She had been a challenge. Like he said—
something different. It was his pride that was wounded
now; his heart—if he had a heart—was quite intact.

She stood very still as she stared into his furious face,
and after a full thirty seconds she said quietly, 'I
wouldn't hurt Emma. That would be the very last thing
I would want.'

'I don't believe you,' he said with icy coldness.

'Then perhaps it's best if I leave immediately, so my
foul presence doesn't contaminate her in any way?'
Tamar said with sudden bitter savagery, knowing if she
didn't begin to hit back, to retreat, she would collapse
in a broken heap at his feet. And no way was she going
to give him that satisfaction.

'And don't act the offended innocent; it doesn't suit
you.' He glared at her, the explosive rage he was trying

to keep in check evident in the dark fury in his face and
the hard, uncompromising tautness of his body. 'You
played me perfectly, dammit, and that took some doing.
Where did you learn all the tricks that kept me dangling
on your hook, Tamar?'

'I didn't learn anything.' She stared at him, her dark
brown eyes velvet-soft with anguish, but if anything her
distress seemed to make him more angry.

'*Stop acting the part,*' he ground out violently. 'It's
over, don't you see that? You've been found out; the
smokescreen is finished with. It's time for the real Tamar
McKinley to take a bow.'

'I hate you.' The words were wrenched out of her
bitter pain and despair, but as she turned to make for the
door he caught hold of her, his fingers steel-like on her
wrist, bruising the soft flesh.

'You hate me?' The savage sarcasm was biting. 'Now
that's probably the first honest thing you've said all
morning. I know you hate me, Tamar, you've always
hated me, haven't you? That's what all this is about.'

'Yes, yes...' She would have said anything now, in
her desire to get away from him before she broke down
completely.

'But you were prepared to let me hold you, kiss you,
touch you, nevertheless,' he spat disgustedly. 'Did I
make your flesh creep? Was it as bad as that? Or did it
excite you, knowing you had me under your spell and
that you were in control? How far were you prepared to
go, Tamar, in this plan of revenge? All the way?' he
finished with bitter condemnation.

'Let go of me!' She was twisting and turning in his
hold, like a beautiful fiery-haired bird caught in an un-
relenting snare.

'Perhaps I don't want to.' Her head jerked up at his deadly cold voice. 'Perhaps I want to see how much was acting on your part and how much was real. Shall we see, Tamar? Shall we see how much was real?' he asked with grim intent. 'I don't doubt for a moment that you are an experienced and accomplished lover; that little scene you put on for me last night in the kitchen was good, very good. Were you enjoying our lovemaking— in spite of the loathing you have for me as a person— or were you merely enduring what had to be endured? I'm really very interested to find out,' he finished with sardonic darkness.

'Don't you dare. Don't you *dare*—'

'Don't tell me what to do, Tamar, not any more. You provoke and entice, and you know exactly what you're doing, don't you?' He pulled her into him, still holding her by the wrist but with one arm now securely round her waist. 'It's all "no", and "please stop", isn't it? But not any more.'

The kiss was a savage exercise in subjugation, and Tamar knew a terror so great that she was frozen and helpless in his grasp. He was a stranger, this fierce, angry man in Jed's body, and the years fell away like magic. That same sense of defenceless exposure, the sheer brute strength over her feebleness, caused her to panic in animal-like distress, and as before she began to fight her tormentor in any way she could.

And then it all changed. His mouth became persuasive rather than ruthless, and although he was still holding her against him, in a way that made her aware of every inch of his hard, demanding body, he was kissing her in a way that she could enjoy. His exploration of her mouth was voluptuous and teasingly erotic, and he took his time, building slowly on her arousal moment by moment until her legs were fluid and her trembling apparent to both of them.

He made a hoarse, growling sound deep in his throat, and there was an immediate echo in her body. She wanted him. But he mustn't know, she couldn't... What she couldn't do became hopelessly lost in the touch and taste and smell of him, her senses blanketed by a warm, aching desire that spiralled her into another dimension.

Some time in the last few minutes her hands had crept up to his shoulders, and the hard-muscled flesh beneath soft silk was another source of pleasure, causing her to press her softness against the hard ridge of his body as she moaned softly.

When he sank down to the carpet she went with him willingly, blindly, her breathing ragged and her face flushed with fierce desire as he continued the wickedly experienced, hungry assault on her body. His hands and lips were compelling, his finesse absolute, and he sensed the capitulation her passion was inducing, responding to it with another little growl.

'Tell me you want me, Tamar. Say it,' he groaned thickly. 'I need to know. Say you want me now.'

'Oh, Jed, I do, I do. I love you,' she murmured rapturously.

And then she knew instantly what she had said, as the white-hot desire that had him as hard as a rock froze, and he lifted himself to stare down into her drowning eyes. 'No, no dressing it up with meaningless words,' he said harshly. 'Say it as it is. Be honest for once. You *want* me. Say it.'

She stared back at him, too shattered to move or speak.

'Say it,' he ordered again, the silver-grey eyes holding hers like pinpoints of glittering steel. 'Say it, Tamar.'

And then, when she still continued to look at him, returning reason sending her into a black hole of misery, his mouth twisted contemptuously. 'You can't face the fact that a man you loathe can make you feel the way I make you feel, can you?' he said bitterly. 'But I'm not playing any more games, Tamar. You don't love me, we both know that, but you want me physically. Fine.'

'No…' It was a soft whimper, and his eyes narrowed before he shook his head slowly.

'Still keeping up the pretence?' His voice was husky, the grating quality underlined when he continued, 'I only have to touch you again to prove what we both know.'

He thought she was denying her physical attraction to him, she thought painfully, not refuting his statement about her lack of love. She struggled up into a sitting position, smoothing down her clothes and dropping her gaze from his, but he reached for her again, only pausing when there was a gentle, tentative knock at the study door.

He swore once, harshly, under his breath, before calling, 'Just a moment,' and rising swiftly to his feet, hauling her up a moment later. She watched him as he tucked his midnight-blue silk shirt back into the waistband of his jeans, his derisively raised eyebrows preparing her for his cynical parting shot of, 'Saved by the bell—or in this case, I suspect, Emma.'

And then, to her shock and amazement, she watched him unlock the study door. *He had locked it.* She felt too crushed to react. He had purposely made sure they couldn't be interrupted, and that meant… That meant he had determined to make love to her all along. It had been to prove a point, to demonstrate to her that she was putty in his hands.

The devastating humiliation gave way to fierce, burning anger, and as Jed opened the door to reveal Emma in the hall outside Tamar's chin came up and her back stiffened. He had made it clear he didn't want her here, near his sister, and that was fine, but there was no way she was assuaging his injured male ego by letting him take her body before she was unceremoniously turned out of his home and his life.

How dared he—how *dared* he—assume she would fall into his hands like a ripe peach? He had been right in describing himself as a monster, she thought bitterly. It was liquid ice flowing through his veins—not blood.

'Is...is everything all right?' Emma's voice was hesitant, her eyes flashing from her brother's face to where Tamar was still standing in the middle of the room. 'Ronald didn't say anything to offend Tamar, did he?'

And then her previous theory was blown away, as Tamar watched Jed bend over the wheelchair and say, very tenderly, 'Come on through to the dining room and have something to eat. You're seeing Colin later, and it wouldn't do to faint on the poor guy. And don't worry about Ronald—he's gone and he's not coming back, okay?' he said firmly. 'He's out of your life for good, Emma.'

'Okay.' Emma nodded, and then peered round her brother to Tamar, saying, 'You're all right, Tamar?'

'Fine.' Tamar forced a bright smile.

'Thank you for not letting him in,' Emma said quietly. 'I know it's cowardly, but I really don't want to see him again.'

'Far from being cowardly, I think it shows remarkably

good sense,' Tamar said stoutly, and this time her smile wasn't forced as she added, 'You're doing fine, Emma.'

'No, not really, but I'm getting there. Colin...Colin helps,' Emma admitted shyly, turning her wheelchair to face the dining room as she spoke, her cheeks flushing.

Tamar followed the other two through to breakfast purely for Emma's sake. She didn't want to upset the other girl by insisting on going to her room, although she knew exactly what she was going to do once Colin had arrived to take Emma out.

Breakfast proved to be an ordeal Tamar wouldn't have wished on her worst enemy. Jed managed to be an attentive big brother to Emma—all charm and wry, amusing comments—at the same time as making Tamar feel she was something he would scrape off the bottom of his shoe.

But he was clever with it, Tamar told herself bitterly, after another pointed comment had found its target. Emma clearly didn't suspect a thing. He could act a part to perfection.

'Not hungry, Tamar?' As she raised her head Jed gestured to the piece of toast on her plate that she had been nibbling at for a good five minutes. 'You need some exercise to give you an appetite. I'll have to see what I can do after breakfast.'

'Go for a swim, Tamar,' Emma encouraged innocently. 'I've already had a dip this morning, and the water is lovely and warm. Jed keeps it at just the right temperature.'

Bully for Jed. She kept her face bland and her voice light as she said, 'I might do that later, after my meal has gone down.'

'Hardly a meal.' Jed's eyes were laser-sharp even as

his mouth smiled—a shark smile, Tamar thought wildly. 'You've only had half a piece of toast and a bowl of grapefruit.'

'I don't often eat breakfast,' Tamar said stiffly.

Jed was just opening his mouth for what Tamar was sure was another barbed comment coated in sugar, when Mrs Trotter popped her head round the door. 'Mr Cannon, I'm sorry to disturb you, but that call you've been waiting for from Australia? They're on the line now,' the housekeeper said cheerfully.

'Right, I'll take it in my study, Mrs Trotter.' He rose slowly, his face warm as he nodded at Emma, and then the temperature dropped by twenty degrees as he glanced Tamar's way. 'I'll see you later.' It was a threat, not a promise.

'Oh, take as long as you like,' Tamar said brightly. 'I've a good book to read, so I thought I'd take it down by the pool and relax a little before my swim.'

He nodded, his face dark and brooding and his eyes hooded. 'Hadn't you better get ready for Colin?' he asked Emma carefully. 'He'll be here in a few minutes and Tamar won't mind.'

He couldn't have made it clearer he didn't trust her to be alone with his sister, Tamar thought balefully, feeling herself flush bright red with anger, but unable to do anything about it other than pretend to drop her napkin under the table. She fished about under the thick linen tablecloth for some moments and then emerged slowly, hoping Emma would leave the room with Jed. She did, after a warm goodbye to Tamar that made Tamar feel a little guilty in view of what she had decided to do.

But it was the only possible option, she reassured herself a few moments later as she sped up to her room, her heart pounding and her stomach churning. She had to leave here. *Now*. This morning. She would wait until Colin had taken Emma out—he was due to arrive in five minutes and they were planning a shopping excursion followed by lunch—and then, once the coast was clear, she would ring for a taxi and leave.

She packed her small suitcase with frenzied haste, and, after hearing Colin arrive, telephoned for a taxi. Colin and Emma left the house a few moments later, and Tamar gave a deep sigh of relief. The last thing she wanted was a confrontation with Jed on the doorstep, with Emma and Colin looking on.

But there was no confrontation. Tamar watched for the taxi to arrive from her vantage point upstairs, and then flew down to the hall on silent feet, opening the front door and slipping out before closing it very quietly behind her.

She didn't breathe easily until the taxi was out of the big gates at the end of the drive and heading towards her flat, and then reaction set in and she began to shiver and shake. It was over—not that it had ever really begun—and it had finished in the worst possible way. He hated her, and, even worse, despised her. Why hadn't she told him about Mike Goodfellow and explained that she had been telling the truth about the last five years? But he hadn't given her the chance, she told herself tremblingly. Although perhaps if she had said—

Stop it. Stop it. The reprimand was sharp in her head. It wouldn't have made any difference. If he had loved her, if he had even had some tender affection for her—anything—there might have been a chance. But a chance of what? To be one of his women for a while, to live in hope that he might, just might, change his mind about marriage and lifelong commitment? Who was she fooling? she asked herself miserably. He was as he was, and it would have killed her to live like that—waiting, hoping, dreading the moment he tired of her body and wanted out.

No, it had had to end. She hugged her middle as the ache in her heart became excruciating. But she didn't know how she was going to get through the rest of her life.

She was almost back to the flat when another thought penetrated the black misery, causing her to sit bolt upright and clutch nervously at her throat. What if he followed her here and demanded what he saw as payment for the dance she had led him? He was angry enough. She closed her eyes at the thought, her nerves jumping. She wouldn't be able to stand it. She had to get away for a time, give him a chance to cool down and see that she wasn't going to contact Emma or do anything else to hurt his sister. That was all he was really bothered about anyway.

She breathed deeply, willing herself to think clearly. She still had several weeks' holiday owing this year, and money wasn't a problem—the commission on Greenacres had put her bank balance very firmly in the black, much to her bank manager's delight. But she didn't want to go to some strange place; the thought of a holiday in the sun didn't appeal any more somehow. She'd go and spend some time with Gaby.

Once the thought was there, it clarified immediately. Yes, that was what she'd do. She needed to be with someone who cared about her, weak though that might be. Someone who knew what she was *really* like. The flood of self-pity threatened to overwhelm her, and she blinked back the tears determinedly. She'd brought this on herself; that was what she had to remember. She deserved his low opinion of her.

When the taxi stopped outside the flat, she asked the driver if he would wait and then take her to King's Cross station. 'No problem, ducks.' He was as round as he was tall, with a rosy red face and beaming smile. 'You want any help with bags, anything like that?' he offered cheerily.

She started to refuse—since the attack she had been meticulously careful never to be alone with a man or put herself in an awkward situation—but then she paused. Somewhere, sometime, she had to start trusting the male population again— she couldn't lump them all together with scum like Mike Goodfellow.

'It's all right, ducks. I've got three kids of me own, and the eldest is about your age,' the taxi driver said reassuringly. 'Lives by herself in a bedsit in Birmingham, and the wife and me are always tellin' her to be on her guard. The things you hear these days…'

Tamar nodded, looking into the bright, round button eyes that reminded her of a robin's. 'I've got to get a few things together, but the case will be quite heavy,' she said quietly. 'If you could help me get it down the stairs, that would be a help.'

The telephone was ringing when Tamar opened the front door of the flat but she let it ring. She would phone Fiona and Richard *en route*; she knew they wouldn't mind her taking two or three weeks' leave when she explained the circumstances. They had been nagging her to have a holiday for ages. And she'd phone her aunt too—if they couldn't put her up for any reason she could always stay in a bed and breakfast somewhere close. But for now she wanted to leave the flat quickly—once she did that, she was safe.

She bundled clothes, books, toiletries and anything else she thought she might need higgledy-piggledy into her enormous old suitcase, tipping the contents of the overnight case she had taken to Jed's on top of it all, before shutting the case quickly.

The taxi driver was waiting in the hall, and the little round face beamed at the sight of her. 'Blimey, girl, I wish the wife'd pack as quick as that,' he said approvingly, taking the case from her and then adding over his shoulder, 'Has the house in an uproar for days, my missus, and still we end up forgettin' somethin' essential.'

She was finding the little man very comforting, but his kindness was making her want to cry. She felt so emotionally bruised, so drained and totally shattered, that she couldn't imagine ever feeling like herself again. But she would—she would, she told herself numbly. She'd managed it once before, after all.

And then she was in the back of the taxi again, only relaxing when it had left Crayfrield Avenue and turned into the anonymity of mainstream traffic.

Tamar didn't know what made her glance out of the window some minutes later—perhaps a sixth sense, female intuition—but as the taxi crawled along in the heavy Saturday traffic her eyes fastened on the stationary line of vehicles on the other side of the road, waiting for the traffic lights to change.

He was driving the Ferrari. And even from a distance of some few yards she could see the furious darkness of his face and the way the big body was tensed over the steering wheel. He didn't notice her—there was no reason he should; taxis were ten a penny in London—and she feasted her eyes on him for long, heartbreaking moments before the lights changed and the Ferrari growled away.

Her tears were blinding her now, hot, scorching tears of remorse and regret and piercing pain, but by the time the taxi arrived at King's Cross she had regained enough shaky composure to thank the taxi driver and give him a hefty tip, before making her way to the information desk to enquire the time of the train. The train that would take her away from London, away from Jed Cannon, and into a future where she could only see darkness and grief and deep, grinding misery.

CHAPTER NINE

TAMAR stayed away for a full three weeks, returning to London on a wild, wet November day that blew her hair into a cascade of bright red-gold curls her clips couldn't contain and put healthy colour into her cheeks. But the outward appearance of vibrant colour and life was an illusion, she admitted silently, as she caught sight of herself in the wardrobe mirror after dumping her suitcase on the bed. Inside she was grey.

Gaby had been wonderful, hiding her horrified surprise at what Tamar had done after one shocked, 'Oh, Tamar,' and then being there when Tamar needed some company without intruding on Tamar's desire for solitude. And she *had* needed to be by herself, Tamar thought now, clicking open the suitcase and beginning to unpack.

She had laid a lot of ghosts during the three weeks' retreat to Scotland, some of which she had been unaware of until she had begun to search her heart and her soul with brutal honesty. Her new state of mind didn't help the grinding loneliness which had grown day by day since she had walked out of Jed's life, nor the overwhelming sense of guilt and shame that had had her pacing the floor until the early hours most nights, but she was glad she had faced the demons of the past nevertheless.

She had realised she had been punishing Mike

Goodfellow when she had aimed to get even with Jed—it hadn't been Gaby she was thinking of, not really.

Jed's apparent ruthlessness with her cousin, his cruel assumption as to Gaby's morals and behaviour, had touched something elemental that had been screaming inside her own brain for five years. She had merely dressed it up as a crusade for Gaby, that was all, Tamar thought bleakly.

After unpacking her things, Tamar made herself some toast and tea and took her tray through to the sitting room, drawing the deep rosey-red curtains before she sat down in front of the welcoming glow of the gas fire. The rain was lashing against the window, an early dusk making it quite dark outside although it was only just after four o'clock.

Tamar ate the toast determinedly—her appetite was non-existent; she had already lost nearly half a stone in the last three weeks, and her clothes were beginning to hang on her— gazing into the flickering fire as she munched. She had come to several decisions in the caustic aftermath of her last confrontation with Jed, and now she reviewed them as dispassionately as she could.

She had lost any chance she might have had with him— completely, utterly—and she felt in her bones she would never fall in love again. So, she had to think her life anew.

If all hope of a husband and family was gone, then she wanted to *do* something with her life, something rewarding. She needed a point to what had become an existence, and working for Fiona and Richard didn't even begin to fulfil that—dear though her friends were.

When she had first gone to university she had had the idea of a career in social services, working with needy families and especially children, but Mike Goodfellow had caused her to lose all confidence in herself and her ability to cope with the pressures such a career would involve. But her degree was a good one. She nodded to herself in the quiet room. So it was up to her—it was all up to her. And she wasn't going to hide away any longer.

When the knock came at her front door, Tamar's brow wrinkled before she suddenly realised who it was. Of course—she had told Fiona and Richard when she was expected back, and, knowing Fiona, she had come round to check all was well.

She padded out to the hall, stitching a determinedly bright smile on her face as she opened the door. Only it wasn't Fiona. Or Richard. It wasn't Tim either.

'Hallo, Tamar.' The deep voice was cool and expressionless.

Her reaction wasn't at all cool, but as she swung the door shut he was too quick for her, an expensive Italian leather shoecap diving onto the threshold and wedging the door open.

He looked wonderful, she thought desperately, big, dark and handsome, and the slight dampness from the ferociously wet weather outside was causing his hair to fall over his forehead in what was almost a quiff. It gave a boyishness to the hard, handsome face that was dynamite, and she knew her voice was shaky when she whispered, 'What are you doing here?'

'Looking for you,' he said softly. And then, as her hand went to her throat in nervous apprehension, he said, 'It's all right, it's all right, I'm not going to hurt you.' And in that moment she knew, with an intuition made all the more sensitive because of her love for him, that somehow he had found out about Mike Goodfellow. Her heart stopped, and then raced furiously.

He was feeling sorry for her. It was worse than all the pain of the last three weeks, and Tamar's soft mouth tightened, her back straightening as she said again, 'What are you doing here?' her voice hostile.

'I thought you might like to know how Emma's last appointment went?' he said quietly, with a faint air of reproach.

'Oh...yes, of course.' It wasn't what she had expected. 'I...I'm sorry, of course I want to know. How...? What did the doctors say?' she stammered weakly, knowing she couldn't keep him standing on the doorstep when he had called to tell her such momentous news, but utterly unable to find the courage to invite him into the flat either.

Jed solved her problem by the simple expedient of stepping forward, so she was forced to step back into the hall, whereby he followed her into the flat, shutting the door after him, and then staring down at her from wary, watchful eyes. 'It went very well,' he said simply. 'The treatment has been an unmitigated success. There is no reason why she shouldn't live a full, active and very long life once she has recovered her strength.'

'Oh, Jed, I'm so pleased.' And she was, but she still couldn't rid herself of the impression that he knew. 'That's...that's wonderful news,' she said shakily.

'And she's going to make an honest man of Colin once her divorce from Ronald comes through,' Jed continued steadily. 'She's already looking for a house in the suburbs big enough to take Colin and all his books, as well as the quiver full of kids she intends to have, so I'll be looking for a new housemate soon.'

He smiled, but for the life of her Tamar couldn't smile back. Was this how the other half lived? she thought helplessly. Could the cool, sophisticated beauties Jed was normally involved with take the sort of scene they had endured and carry on as though nothing had happened? But then she doubted if any other woman had dared to do what she had done. The thought brought a moment of nervous hysteria, but then his next words washed it away like a bucket of cold water.

'I'm sorry, Tamar,' he said quietly.

'What?' Please don't let him know, she prayed desperately. I'll do anything, anything, if he doesn't know. She couldn't bear his pity—his hate was better than that.

Her prayers were in vain.

'I followed you here the morning you ran away from me,' he said steadily, still making no effort to touch her. 'But you had already left. I went crazy for a time, then— raging about like a bull in a china shop—and, not surprisingly, Fiona and Richard wouldn't tell me where you'd gone. I think they thought I meant to hurt you.'

Hurt her? Oh, he'd hurt her all right, Tamar thought painfully, but not by anything he had said or done. He had made her fall in love with him—what could be worse than that? 'I had some holiday to take,' she said stiffly.

'I know, Fiona said that much—along with telling me I was the biggest idiot on the earth,' he said flatly.

'She didn't? Fiona didn't say that, did she?' Tamar asked incredulously. The Cannon business was very important to Fiona and Richard's fledgling enterprise, and they still hadn't made a sale on his apartment. It said a lot for the strength of Fiona's affection for her that her friend would put their friendship before her precious

child, Tamar thought wryly, the knowledge warming her
for a few brief seconds before Jed spoke again.

'She was right.' He was wearing his poker face, but
there was something deep in the beautiful silver eyes that
was causing the breath to constrict in her throat, and the
feeling of uneasiness to increase tenfold. 'Anyway, I
tried threats, bribery—all the sorts of tactics you would
expect from a man like me—' the edge of dark humour
didn't make her smile '—and then I decided that as you
knew everything about me, it was only right and proper
I did some investigating of my own.'

She shut her eyes for a split second as a terrible sense
of inevitability engulfed her. 'I...I don't know what you
mean.'

'I think you do.' She made no reply to this, but her
eyes were the eyes of a trapped animal and her face was
chalk-white.

'Why didn't you tell me, Tamar?' he asked softly,
knowing he had to go slowly, that the slender, fragile
girl in front of him was at the end of her tether. 'Did
you think I wouldn't understand? Was that it? Or that
I'd blame you in some way, think less of you—?'

'Please go. I want you to go.' Her heart was shaking
her ribcage with its frightened panicked beats. What did
he expect— that she would now discuss this with him?
Was that it? Because she couldn't; she couldn't discuss
it with anyone—not ever. If he had loved her it would
still have been impossible, but thinking of her as he did,
it was inconceivable.

'I'm not going anywhere.' And then, as she began to
tremble, he said softly, 'Sit down, Tamar. I just want to
talk for a while, that's all.'

'There's no point,' she murmured shakily, 'you must

see that? We...we said all that could be said that Saturday morning three weeks ago.'

'We said nothing that was real then,' he bit back sharply, and then, as she flinched at his tone, added, 'Please, sit down.'

She sat. It was either that or falling in a trembling little heap at his feet, and that really would be the final humiliation. She didn't know what to do or what to say, and she felt such panic and despair that it was like the court case all over again.

'I know this isn't easy for you.' He was even using the language the lawyers had used, she thought hysterically, bowing her head and biting on her lip to stop herself from screaming at him to stop. 'And I've made it a damn sight harder, haven't I?'

'What?' She did look at him then, struck by the ragged pain in his voice, and he sat down opposite her as she did so, his hands hanging loosely between his knees and his eyes looking straight into hers.

'The things I accused you of...' He paused. 'I didn't understand, Tamar, I didn't *know*,' he said with painful self-disgust.

Oh, God, please make him stop this, she prayed helplessly. I don't want his pity or his good intentions. If he couldn't love her that was one thing, but this...

'Do you want to talk about it?' he asked softly. 'Tell me in your own words?'

'*No.*' Panic made her voice fierce. 'No, I don't.'

'No matter. I can wait until you're ready,' he said calmly.

Why that simple sentence was the catalyst for the flood of rage and pain and loss that flooded her system, Tamar didn't know, but she took them both by surprise

when she sprang to her feet, her eyes wild as she
shouted, 'I don't want you to wait, don't you see? And
I don't want you to feel sorry for me either! I'm not a
victim, Jed. I'm not. I've built a life for myself. I'm not
a little waif and stray that needs your charity, so you
can just get out. Go back to your wheeling and dealing,
and your...your wom—women.'

She hadn't wanted to cry. That thought was uppermost
as the wild sobs that racked her body burst forth from
her eyes, her nose, her mouth, the tension of the last
three weeks and his sudden appearance proving too
much.

She tried to struggle when he took her in his arms,
but his grip tightened, his arms strong but curiously gentle as he held her until the worst of the storm was spent.

'You've been brave. You've been very brave, my darling.' He had been muttering incoherent words of comfort but now, as his words penetrated her misery, she
jerked in his hold, pushing at his chest with shaking
hands as she tried to free herself.

'I don't want you to feel sorry for me.' It was a wail
of despair. 'And I don't want to ever see you again. Just
leave me alone. Please, Jed, leave me alone.'

'I can't.' He was breathing hard, his face as white as
a sheet and his eyes black with pain. 'I love you.'

Tamar closed her eyes, anguish tearing through her
and making her feel as though she was disintegrating
into a tiny speck of nothingness. 'You don't believe in
love,' she said with trembling dignity. 'You know you
don't. That Saturday when you found out what I'd done
you were disgusted with me, you wanted me far away
from Emma—'

'No, it was you who decided to leave,' he said gently.

'I admit I reacted badly—' he took a deep, hard breath before continuing '—but I'm no saint, Tamar. I've never purported to be. I handled it all wrong, I know that—I knew it from the first moment I found you gone—and I have no excuse. I lost my temper. For the first time in a long, long time I lost my temper. There was the great Jed Cannon, the man who has it all under control, all at his fingertips, and suddenly I didn't know if I was coming or going. I'd lost it,' he added shakily.

'You hated me,' she whispered, her voice barely audible.

'No, I loved you,' he corrected softly. 'But you didn't love *me*, and that's what my bull-headed pride couldn't take. For the first time in my life I wasn't in control. *I* was dancing to *your* tune, and I was furious with myself—and you—for making me feel like that. I'd walked on eggshells for weeks, tried everything I knew, and still you were holding out on me.'

'You mean I wouldn't go to bed with you,' she said dully. This wasn't real. She didn't, *couldn't* trust that it was real.

'Tamar, look at me,' he said huskily. 'Please?' She raised her head and opened wary eyes to see his dark face just inches from hers. 'I admit at first, right at the beginning, my sole aim was to get you into bed,' he acknowledged quietly. 'And part of my love is made up of sexual desire; I can't help that. But only part, understand? If I have to wait until that side of things feels right for you, I'll wait—however long it takes. Maybe not patiently—' he smiled, but she couldn't smile back '—but I'll wait none the less. Because I love *you*, all of you, not just your body or a performance in bed. I love your warmth, your tender heart, your sense of humour, your purity—'

And now she jerked right out of his arms, her voice wretched as she said, 'I'm not pure, though, am I? You know about...about him—Mike Goodfellow—don't you?'

'Yes, I know.' There was a grimness to his voice that had been absent before. 'And if he wasn't already dead, he'd have wished he was after I'd finished with him.'

'He's dead?' She stared at him open-mouthed. 'Mike Goodfellow is dead?' She didn't feel any of the emotions she would have expected at such news, merely an overwhelming relief that there was no chance she would ever see him again.

'Heart attack,' Jed said tightly, 'while he was still in prison. And, frankly, it couldn't have happened to a nicer guy. Retribution isn't always that swift, but in his case it wasn't a day too late. And listen to me, Tamar.' He took hold of her upper arms, his grip firm but gentle as he looked straight into her drenched eyes. 'You are as pure and untouched to me as the day you were born. Gaby's told me how hard it's been for you to come to terms with what happened for the last five years—'

'Gaby?' This was fast becoming surreal, Tamar thought bewilderedly, feeling her grip on reality lessening by the minute. 'How have you spoken to Gaby?'

'I telephoned her a few days after you'd left, when I managed to get hold of her number,' Jed admitted sheepishly. 'There was a faint possibility you might have gone there, instead of abroad, as Fiona had hinted—' his raised eyebrows expressed his opinion of Fiona's deviousness '—and I wanted to know where you were. I was worried about you. She wouldn't speak to me at first, but I crawled a bit—' never, Tamar thought in disbelief. Never in a month of Sundays '—and she admitted you were with her, but that you needed time to sort things out—things that had been hanging around for years.'

'I don't believe this,' Tamar said weakly. 'She didn't say a word to me.' She didn't know whether to be upset at Gaby's scheming or touched by her cousin's love for her.

'She said if I cared anything about you, I wouldn't barge in and confuse the issue,' Jed continued quietly. 'I care, so...'

Tamar shook her head, her throat closing with fear. She didn't believe him; she couldn't believe him. Jed Cannon could have any woman he wanted, so why should she be the one he fell in love with? He might not be aware of it, but he *was* feeling sorry for her—she had seen him with Emma; she knew that hard shell had a soft centre—but pity wasn't enough. It wouldn't last. One day he would tire of her, as he had tired of all the others.

'Jed, please go,' she whispered brokenly. 'If you do care about me even a little bit, please go.'

'No.' It was unequivocal. 'You said, that last morning, you said...you loved me. When you weren't thinking with your head, keeping up your guard, you said you loved me, Tamar. It's been the only thing that has prevented me from "barging in", as Gaby put it, because for you to say that, being the sort of person you are, you meant it, and I could trust you enough to wait.'

Tamar stared at him. She couldn't move. She couldn't think. And she needed to. She needed to deflect the question she knew he was going to ask, the question she could read in the mercurial silver-grey of his eyes.

'Do you love me?' It was quiet, but there was a little tremble in the words that told her he wasn't as sure of her as he would like her to believe, and it touched her as nothing else could have done.

She wasn't aware she was crying again until he reached out a tentative hand and brushed her cheek gently. 'Do you, Tamar?' he persisted softly. 'It's the only thing that matters now.'

'It doesn't make any difference,' Tamar prevaricated helplessly. 'You think you've got to prove to me that you still want me in spite of the...the rape, but I don't expect that sort of chivalry, Jed. And I haven't changed my mind about not having an affair with you either. I couldn't—I just couldn't. I'm not made that way. It's got nothing to do with what happened at university; it's *me*.'

'Do you think I don't know that?' he bit back, with such fury in his voice that she stepped back a pace, totally taken aback. 'I know you couldn't have an affair with me—damn it all, I know that. And I don't want a brief liaison with you either. I love you, dammit, and I want to marry you. I want you to be the mother of my children; I want to see you with our grandchildren—when that beautiful hair of yours is white and you still look as breathtaking as ever. *I love you, Tamar.* I love *you.*'

She should say something. Tamar knew she should say something. But she felt caught inside a rushing spiral of feeling that was taking her she knew not where.

'I don't know how to prove it to you,' Jed said after a full thirty seconds had ticked by, when they had simply looked into each other's faces, and his voice was calmer now.

'Especially in view of the stupid things I've said. But if it takes months, years, I'll make you believe me, Tamar. If I don't marry you, I shan't marry anyone; I know that now. That garbage I said...' He shook his head. 'I won't marry anyone. I mean it. I'll simply wait and hope until the day you change your mind,' he finished with magnificent humbleness.

'Don't...don't do this.' The whirlwind of emotion was taking her upwards, towards the light, but it was hurting—it was hurting so much, more than she could bear.

'You're my lady, Tamar. You're all mine. In here, where it counts.' He placed his fist across his heart. 'You are everything I've ever dreamt of, everything I could ever have hoped for—my perfect, beautiful, miraculous lady.'

Through a haze of tears she looked at him, and now the feeling was flooding every inch of her body, making her light-headed as hope surged deep inside.

'I'll show you how to learn to trust me,' he continued, with a sensitivity that belied the cold, ruthless image he showed the world. 'Every day, for the rest of our lives, I'll be there for you. Nothing will come before you, Tamar—not my work, my friends, family—not even our children. You will come first. You'll always come first. That's my promise to you.'

And then she was in the light, in a sudden, swooping rush, and she realised it was really that easy. He loved her. She loved him. The rest didn't matter. Her traumatic past, his bitter disillusionment with life and love—it was all gone, burnt up in the healing fire of this all-consuming *precious* love they shared. She loved him and he was hers.

Her senses were reeling, but through the dizzy wonder

of it she was aware of his face, dark and compelling, as he willed her to believe him.

'I'm not going to stop asking you to marry me.' He had clearly mistaken her stunned, wide-eyed wonder at the revelation which had burst forth in her soul as a prelude to refusal, and he took her hands in his, willing her to listen. 'I know too well I've made a pig's ear of all this, and you don't believe me, but you will. I'll make you. I'm not going to go away, Tamar, whatever you say or do. I'm going to keep knocking on the door of your heart until it opens again and you tell me what you told me that Saturday. I shan't give in.'

'Jed—'

'I've been searching for you all my life without realising it,' he said huskily. 'You're my other half; you're *part* of me. I can't let you go. You're what I was created for.'

'*Jed.*'

And now he did stop talking, and she recognised—with a stab of love that took her breath away—the vulnerability that was staring out of his eyes as he waited for her to speak. This big, hard, handsome man, this giant in the world of finance, who had more power and wealth and success than the average man could dream of, was just the same as any other emotionally bruised human being. Just as fearful of rejection.

'I love you, Jed,' she said softly. 'I've always loved you. I was born loving you...'

His whole body tautened for one endless moment, and then she was in his arms, without any clear idea of how she had got there. The kiss was long and hard and desperate, and his mouth left hers only to cover her eyes, her nose, her throat, in little scorching kisses as he held her crushed against him.

'Does that mean yes?' he asked long minutes later, when they both came up for air, his voice stifled and gruff with the passion that held him in its grip. 'You'll marry me?'

'If you're sure...' Tamar murmured dazedly.

'Sure?' He looked down into her starry eyes, his face saying all she needed to hear. 'I've never been so sure of anything in my life. I want to spend every second, every moment with you.'

'What about your business empire? You won't be able to devote yourself to it in the same way,' she warned tremulously. 'Especially when we have children.'

'What business empire? I've forgotten it already.'

'And your friends? What if they don't like me?' she persisted softly, leaning back in his arms to see his face more clearly.

'Tough.' He pulled her closer. 'But they'll love you. How could they not love you? Anyway—' he shook his head irritably '—what the hell are we thinking about other people for at a time like this? I don't care about anyone else, only you, and you only care about me.' The arrogance was pure Cannon, but Tamar had to admit he was absolutely right.

But there was still one hurdle she had to face. She had to tell him it all—talk about the rape in all its ugliness and look at his face as she did so. It was the only way she could go forward into this new life that was beckoning in his eyes.

'Jed, I need to tell you...' She paused, her voice breaking.

'No, not if you don't want to,' he said urgently. 'Tamar, I love you. It only matters to me in so much as it matters to you—'

'I need to tell you,' she said again, her voice firmer now as she drew on his love and support.

It wasn't easy, and both their faces were awash with tears by the time she had finished, but they were cleansing tears, born of hope and love rather than pain and misery, and he held her close to his heart for long minutes when she had finally stopped talking.

'I meant what I said, my love.' After a while he eased her from him slightly, in order to look into her face, but not before she had felt the desire trembling through the big, muscled body and the power of his masculinity. 'The physical side can wait until you are ready. I want you to need me as much as I need you in every way— mind and soul and body. I want it to be right for you.'

'Jed, you had it all from day one,' Tamar said softly, a tremulous smile quivering her lips.

And then there was no more talking as his mouth sought hers again in hungry, tender homage, the loving reassurance mingling with a rising passion that she knew was for real.

This was her man, this was for ever. Whatever the future held for them—mountaintops of joy and happiness, and maybe the odd valley of tears—they would walk it together. Two hearts, two bodies, two souls united as one.

She was safe; she was home; she was whole.